PROSE FICTION

PROSE FICTION

UEA MA
Creative Writing Anthologies
2019

CONTENTS

Foreword

One thing I've noticed about creative writing courses: people often sign up to them at a hinge moment in their lives, at a pivot or crisis. For some, it's simply entry into adulthood, or a lunge at a new career; for others, a shift has occurred in their soul and they need to find the words for it. Both as a teacher and a student on such courses, I've met my fair share of survivors and seekers: divorcees, retirees, refugees, people in recovery (and, in one memorable instance, an alien abductee); those who've decided to write their way through a personal break, to fix it or perhaps to ensure it stays broken. Announcing that you're throwing it all in to be a writer is an excellent way to signal to the world that you've reached a point of no return. That you want to be new.

I was doing something similar when I came to UEA. By swapping my home in a sunny South African beach city for a Tombland shoebox in the wintry shadow of the cathedral, I was choosing to freeze my real life for three years, to take a look around and decide my next move (while also literally freezing). Norwich befuddled my sense of time, generally. When I did my MA – in another country, another century – I was the youngest writer I knew. In the PhD class, surrounded by brilliant youth, I sometimes felt like the oldest person in any hemisphere. But I was also pleasingly new-hatched: this was the first time I'd ever lived for an extended period in a foreign city, and the one I'd picked was so very, very old.

Despite our differences, I recognised my classmates as fellow hatchlings. We were all perched at the edge of the nest. Some had travelled even more miles to get there than I had; some, I fear, had almost bankrupted themselves to do the course. While some people seemed to arrive fully formed, with international book deals in place and more on the way, everyone was willing themselves into becoming this new thing: a proper writer.

I felt at a relative advantage in that I'd been published before, and so I already knew certain important things about the process, such as: every time you write a book, no matter how many times you do it, you never really know how; at least half of the time it feels like death, and it's impossible to believe that the book is anything but a humiliating catastrophe; and that, nonetheless, you will get the damn thing finished. Yet, despite knowing these things, I had to discover them all over again, as one does with every book. Often I think the best thing a writing mentor can tell you is that this is all to be expected, that others have been through exactly this, and that it will all be OK in the end. You never stop needing to hear it.

And it *was* all OK. We took the stopped time that the degree afforded us and used it to make our own particular breaks with the past and contracts with the future. For a short while we were paused together, absorbed in the long, frozen moment of writing. Then time started up again and we were flung off in a dozen directions – Nigeria, Canada, Singapore, Japan, Colombia, even London; each of us, remarkably, with a manuscript in our hands.

For some of us, this may be the last book we ever write; for others, the first of many. But we all survived our life pivot, and the work we made is the proof.

Just as this book you're holding in your hands is proof: these writers were here together, at a still point in their various lives, as they changed from being one thing to being another. In these stories and extracts, we witness them stepping into the new.

PHILIP LANGESKOV
Introduction

It is a warm Friday in early June and I am in my office looking out over Denys Lasdun's brutalist masterpiece, the UEA campus. In the foreground, the square box of the library gives way to a swatch of green that runs down to the lake; then, the tops of the trees flanking the river Yare, which curls round the western haunch of the campus, carving out a space in the landscape, before flowing east, through the Norfolk Broads, and then out to the sea at Gorleston and whatever lies beyond. From the roof of the library, one of the sculptures from Antony Gormley's *Another Time* series looks out into the early summer air, one of three such life-sized bodyforms placed around the campus. The figures, in Gormley's words, 'freeze time,' and ask 'where the human being sits within the scheme of things'. Standing alone on the library roof, apart from the bustle of living, the figure has the air of someone lost in thought, a dreamer looking off at the distant horizon. The presence of the sculptures around campus has not been without controversy, but I find myself drawn to them, this one in particular. Perhaps it is because I am fond of dreamers; perhaps it is because the figure is there every time I look up from my desk.

On my desk at this precise moment, there is a pile of papers – the printed proof sheets of the book you now hold in your hands. In that pile of papers lies a snapshot of the work undertaken by a group of writers who have come to this campus – from Nigeria, Kenya, Turkey, France, Canada, the US, China, Australia, Austria, Pakistan, and Ireland and all parts of the UK – to devote themselves to the act of placing words on paper. It is not too much of a leap to say that these writers, in coming here, have chosen to freeze time for a while, to step away from the regular flow of living and ask some questions about where the human being sits within the scheme of things. In asking those questions, they have, in their various ways, produced writing of exceptional quality. Writing that enables me, from this Norwich desk and its familiar surroundings, to take a leap into that unfamiliar place where lived experience is transmuted into the broad, unbounded field of fiction. Such transmutations are not easy to make; as the poet Mark Doty has written, 'the world is wily and doesn't want to be caught'. To catch it requires all the obvious things – time, silence, work, talent, luck – but it also requires a willingness to think and, in thinking, to play close attention, both to the self and to the world. In Marilynne Robinson's wonderful novel, *Housekeeping*, there is a passage which seems an apt metaphor both for the way we think and the way we write: 'For why do our thoughts turn to some gesture of a hand, the fall of a sleeve, some corner of a room on a particular anonymous afternoon, even when we are asleep, and even when we are so old that our thoughts have abandoned other business? What are all these fragments for, if not to be knit up finally?'

The writers in these pages are all paying attention, trying to catch the vital fragments that might otherwise slip by – unrecorded, unexamined, forgotten. The evidence of that attention is here in your hands. It emerges from a year of real commitment, during which these writers have attended workshops, masterclasses, tutorials, events of various kinds – not to mention the long hours spent alone at the desk. That commitment, which comes with its shares of euphoria and frustration, is one of the reasons why working with these writers is such a pleasure. There's nothing quite like the feeling of observing a group of writers as they work to bring their stories up from the well of private experience, transforming them into something that can be set down on paper – the paper that is on my desk as I sit here and look out of the window; the paper that is in your hands as you do whatever it is you are doing now.

If I look back to that Gormley figure and attempt to follow its line of sight, it would take me broadly in the direction of the Sainsbury Centre for Visual Arts. Designed by Norman Foster, it houses, among other things, the art collection of Robert and Lisa Sainsbury. At the moment, it is also housing a temporary exhibition: *W. G. Sebald: Far Away – But From Where?* It explores the use of photography in Sebald's work, those uncanny and frequently uncaptioned images that appear often in his books. It is probably not controversial to suggest that these images, these snapshots of frozen time, form an aspect of Sebald's interest in blurring the boundaries between what we know to be true and what we create or imagine – between fact and fiction, in other words. Of course, Sebald was a lecturer here, from 1970, going on to hold a Chair in European Literature and founding the British Centre for Literary Translation (BCLT). Latterly, he also taught on the Prose Fiction MA. Indeed, he delivered his last workshop three days before his death, in December 2001.

Appropriately, for someone so invested in the way the past flows through into the present and the future, Sebald's memory lives on at UEA. The BCLT is still here and hosts the annual Sebald Lecture. A couple of floors below the room in which I currently sit, there is Max's Room, a seminar space for postgraduate students. His books are taught here, notably on a postgraduate module, The Non-Fiction Novel, in which *The Emigrants* rubs up against work by Sheila Heti, Chris Kraus, Ben Lerner and Teju Cole. Also, thanks to two former Prose Fiction students, we can take a glimpse into a Sebaldian creative writing workshop. Robert McGill and David Lambert were both students in Sebald's final workshop group. After his death, they compiled a short treasury of his advice, 'The Collected "Maxims" of W. G. Sebald'. Some of them are straightforward: 'Significant detail enlivens otherwise mundane situations. You need acute, merciless observation.' Others are more complex, requiring some thought to see how they might be applied to a piece of prose: 'Physicists now say there is no such thing as time: everything co-exists. Chronology is entirely artificial and essentially determined by emotion. Contiguity suggests layers of things, the past and present somehow coalescing or co-existing.' There is plenty of mischief – 'I can only encourage you to steal as much as you can' – but there is also plenty of wit and wonder, a reminder that writing is deeply connected to the pleasure of living: 'There has to be a libidinous delight in finding things and stuffing them in your pockets.'

Had he lived on, Sebald would have turned seventy-five last week. It seems appropriate to raise a glass in toast to his memory. And then to raise another one, in toast to the writers in this volume, who chose, for a year or two, to freeze time. They must now release the pause button and make their ways into the future, to find out where their own writing sits in the scheme of things. Here's to them – their presence here has been a pleasure and they are thoroughly deserving of your attention.

This diverse anthology showcases the work of prose writers graduating from UEA's renowned Creative Writing MA and MFA courses in 2019.

Karen Angelico grew up in the Midlands and has a BA in Literature & Art History. She lives in Suffolk with her four sons and works as a digital copywriter. Her first novel, *Everything We Are,* is a dark portrait of two marriages, exploring the emotional and sexual complexities within long-term relationships.

angelicokaren@gmail.com

Everything We Are
An extract from the opening of a novel

Daniel is woken by the sense of her absence. He listens, blinking against the dark, but there is nothing to hear except the ticking of the clock. No cars going past, no barks from the yappy dog two doors down. They used to joke about the alarm dog going off every few hours. A burst of barks, then a high-pitched yelp, as if it was being smacked. He hasn't heard the dog for ages so someone must have had enough. But at least it would be something, to wake with that racket instead. He turns over and tips the clock onto its front.

A line of light glares from under the bottom of the door. He worries about his wife downstairs. She has probably fallen asleep in the chair, half-marked school books slipping from her lap. A drink might be knocked over, spilling on the painted boards, pooling at the edge of the rug. Her late nights are new, and he hasn't yet found a way to negotiate himself around them.

He swings his legs out of bed. The wooden floor is cold on his bare feet and the air cuts into his body. His T-shirt, he realises, is slightly damp across his chest. He reaches for his glasses and inhales sharply. When he went to see his doctor the other week about his twinging back, he was told he should probably lose a few pounds. Maybe he can take up cycling again and go out at weekends with his daughters, once the weather gets warmer.

At the top of the stairs, the light no longer seems as bright. He grips the bannister and edges his feet down the stairwell, feeling his way over the hateful coir carpet. She insisted upon it last year – their final extravagance – and now all the soft carpets have been stripped away. These things are so significant in the middle of the night.

In the sitting room, the standing lamp with the God-awful purple shade throws an aubergine light across the pale walls. It is much warmer down here, although the fire in the wood burner has disappeared to an ashy pile, the roasted smoky smell of it lingering in the air. Kate is curled up in the armchair, asleep and breathing heavily, her head twisted into the corner, her hands tucked between her legs, seeking warmth. He can see a darkened patch of dribble on the brown leather. Perhaps he will point it out to her tomorrow. *That's an easy mark to get out* she will say. But then she will examine the ugly stain and he will know, without even seeing her face, that she is upset.

She stirs a little, burrows further into the corner. Her hair falls over her face and he resists the urge to tuck it behind her ear. It would be silky and smooth in his hand, like a new season conker, fresh out of its case. He knows how it would smell, knows it so well that it would be like smelling his own skin. And he imagines scooping her up, taking her back to bed. They could pretend that whatever has appeared between them doesn't exist.

He wishes she could see this moment. *Look*, he would say. *See how we can be.* Those flashes of mutual loathing are never there when she is asleep, or if he catches her in an off-guard moment. She loses her sharp edges and he can find the truth of her, like he did before.

He wants to know how to get her back.

Earlier, when she was clearing away the dinner things, she said she needed to tell him something. He thought they would finally talk about it – the dark shapeless animal following them around.

She got a glass from the cupboard and went over to the fridge.

'You want one?' she said.

She held up a half-drunk bottle of white wine.

'No thanks,' he said.

She filled her glass almost to the top.

'So?'

It was said like a question she seemed to expect him to understand. He waited.

'So, what's your plan?'

'My plan?'

'Yes, Daniel. Your plan.'

When she said his name, it brimmed with everything he never thought they would become.

'It's been a few months now, and nothing. So, I wondered what exactly *is* your plan? You don't seem to be *doing* anything. You seem quite happy to let this carry on.'

He could have told her about the endless numbers of emails he had written, the hours on the phone, the spreadsheets with every permutation, every conceivable forecast for how long the redundancy money would last. He could have said: *don't worry, we're going to be all right.* After all, that's what he wanted her to say to him.

He said nothing.

She moved her disgusted gaze away from him to the window above the sink. The wind was up, dashing the remaining skeleton heads of dried hydrangea blooms against the outside sill. They both stood, looking out, neither of them moving.

And then: 'I can't fucking well go on like this,' she said, aggressively pushing a strand of hair from her cheek, tucking it behind her ear. 'We'll lose the house you know. We'll lose everything.'

She got all emotional, threw her glass into the sink. It smashed against the side and lay there, like a broken egg. Wine glugged down the plughole.

He can't remember exactly what he said back to her, probably something about how utterly ridiculous she was being. It was always worse whenever he called her hysterical. Maybe he didn't say anything at all. She went off upstairs and he heard her crying in the bathroom.

Kate stirs again, pulling a hand from between her legs and tucking it under her chin. He pauses, although he isn't really sure why he is waiting. The essays she said she had to mark are sitting in a neat, untouched pile on the coffee table, next to a wine glass with a remaining gulp of white. Her laptop is on the floor, balancing at a precarious angle on one of the limp velvet sofa cushions. A bottle is also leaning against the cushion, half-empty. It's not the one she took from the fridge earlier, but the cheap Pinot Grigio he bought at the Spar the other day. He sets the bottle straight and the laptop comes to life, its screen flashing bright. There are two small message windows, side by side with blinking cursors. He kneels down.

Do you know what I'd like to do to you?

I'm sure I can guess...

He scrolls the conversation upwards, the words rolling back. And then the other window:

You're a very naughty girl. I hope you're this naughty when we meet

Who says we're going to meet? I never said we'd meet. How presumptuous you are...

He cannot read any more. The room presses in and he has to stand. He wants to throw the laptop like a Frisbee, watch it crash into the fireplace, smash into pieces on the floor.

She is oblivious, still asleep, her big toe poking through a hole in her tights. The nail is bright pink like those manicured women he used to see on the morning train to work – the women he always avoided, even if it meant he had to stand. Somehow, that toenail is worse than what he has just read.

He leaves everything where it is and takes the stairs at a silent run, reaching the end of the landing without knowing how he got there. His fists are tight knots. His heart knocks against his chest. His breathing is loud and fast. It might explode out of him, this white-hot wordless rage.

Outside his youngest daughter's room, he listens. The door is slightly ajar, and he can hear the sighing breaths of Florence's sleep. He stands in her softness, trying to bring his own breath into line, resting the back of his head on the wall.

When he opens his eyes, he isn't sure how long he's been standing there. Buzzing fills his ears. A numbness in his limbs. He walks with slow and heavy legs back down the corridor.

In the bedroom, there is a shaft of pale silver coming into the room through a gap in the curtains. He goes over to the window and looks out onto the street, at the blank houses opposite. Everything is still, apart from the flicker of dark branches against the moon. The road, which is the main thoroughfare for people coming in and out of the village, is empty. Just the reflected shine of the night sky, glinting from icy crystals starting to form on windscreens and the tops of parked cars. Kate's car is behind his on their narrow drive, bonnet to boot, just fitting on. There is something unnatural about this scene and the dead quiet, as if everything is waiting.

I hope you're this naughty when we meet...

He closes the curtains and sits down on the edge of the bed. The images need to be stuffed away. It helps to grip the edge of the bed and force other thoughts. He is cold, but he doesn't get under the covers. The clock is still face down, the ticking stifled.

The clock. He will think about the clock.

He'd agreed, all those years ago, that it was exactly what they were looking for. They'd gone shopping, not long after they were married, in one of the big department stores on Oxford Street. He had felt in charge that day, taking his new wife around the shops, guiding her with his hand on the small of her back. *Let's buy them,* he'd said, when she showed him a set of brightly coloured drinking glasses. So very different from the son he was used to being, who did what he was told.

That day in the shop, they rode up and down the escalators like they were children allowed to go shopping on their own for the first time. He'd even agreed to take a look at the nursery things on the top floor. She'd picked up tiny socks, pointed out cribs and pushchairs. They'd imagined buying so many things for their new home.

'We can get them another time,' he said when she wanted to buy the clock and a painting with abstract colour splashes. He didn't want to tell her they had no more money to spend.

'I've got this,' she said, reaching into her bag and pulling out an envelope. 'Five hundred and fifty pounds.' She showed him the stack of twenty-pound notes and shoved it back into her bag.

He asked her where she got it and she said her dad had sent it with belated wedding congratulations. She had no idea how the old man had found out, but she said she didn't care. 'It was about time the old bastard actually did something right.'

'We should save it,' he said. He never thought of asking why she hadn't told him about the money before.

'But I want to do something reckless, don't you?' she said. 'I want to remember today as the day we weren't sensible.'

He asked her how her dad knew where to send it and she shrugged. He already knew by then that her shrug meant there was more to it, but he didn't push the topic any further, didn't want to spoil the day. Kate's family and money were two things she didn't like to talk about.

They stood watching the sales assistant cover the painting in layers of bubble wrap. She squeezed his hand and smiled, gave him her special look – the one that made everything feel joyful.

When they got back home, she ran straight upstairs, took everything out of the bags and boxes, put the clock on his bedside table and said they should hang the painting. He stood with his new hammer and pack of nails. She debated which wall to hang it on and he waited for her to decide.

'Perfect,' she said, and they both stood back.

Sussie Anie was born in London to Ghanaian parents. She studied Philosophy, Politics and Economics at the University of Warwick. Her stories blend the speculative with the everyday to explore ideas of home in the transient, and ways in which technology reveals and distorts the human condition. She is the 2018 recipient of the Kowitz Scholarship.

sussieanie@hotmail.com

A Sea of Fake Trees
An extract from a novel

Evander shielded his eyes. Charcoal waters reached everywhere, sparkling with shards of reflected cloud. Ahead, the resort was a smudge where sky and ocean touched.

He crossed his arms against the salt gust. The bulwark's black wood rumbled beneath his elbows as waves nudged the hull. His arms and shoulders shook.

Already, he missed this brine-soaked step; it was the perfect spot for watching. If not for the retreating drizzle, he could see days of ocean in every direction. He had watched the sky braid shadows through the water and seen sunrise after sunrise tease sky and sea apart. Over the past three weeks, he had seen carriers grow from seeds to pompous crafts. He liked to imagine the cities they sailed from and the impenetrable languages their passengers spoke.

The sea looked empty now.

He reached up and dug through his hair. Heat thistled his scalp and burned behind his ears. The itch spread as he rubbed until it was a tight web under his skin, prickling down his neck and back. He saw no point in looking for the bucket to wash, now that the journey was nearly through; he suspected Terra Nullius might be the sort of resort where visitors were required to shave upon arrival.

It might be like the Stone Coast Resort, which ranked among his favourite trips; he'd stayed there exactly two years earlier for his fifteenth birthday. The scent of rain-soaked canvas and leather books came to him now. He could have stayed there all season, reading histories, myths and maps at the Stone Archive House, but Pa only ever sent tokens for ten-day stays.

He pressed the raw skin at his temples. His hair needed cutting. When he'd last worked the knots out, his locks had passed his shoulders. At the very least he could soon wash, with luck, in a Lantic bath: a cavernous, muggy hall where he could soak until his fingertips shrivelled. The thought warmed his chest.

He looked to the shore. There was no denying its colour: beige. Terra

Nullius appeared to be dust. Without luck, it would be barren and crunchy like the Atlantic Haven resort.

His toes curled over the step's splintered edge.

Boots. He ought to find boots. He peered down the ship's length but could not see past the crowd of kids. Fifteen strong: many boys, some girls and more unclear; they were a blur of roast-groundnut faces split by flashes of teeth. They chattered in dialects he did not know.

He turned back to the sea. The air tasted damp with storms unbroken. It held cloying hints of Gup's herbs too, leaking up from below deck. He grinned. Gup was probably rushing to smoke his supply away before they arrived.

More rain was past due. He hoped Terra Nullius's markets were sheltered; without luck they might be like exchange mats back home, where tools and grains lay naked through hail. Freedom to trade would get him nowhere if harsh weather kept crowds thin. He had little to trade, just the tunic on his back and his book of Lantic beasts and birds. He scratched his chin. He had not seen that book in days.

Every gift Pa had sent him was shut in his room at home. The memory of them was a slow ache under his ribs. He imagined his pockets heavy with metal coins, imagined crews of thickset men, yelling to have him join their ships. He saw them waving for him to come aboard. A raider's boy brought luck, everyone knew that.

'Vander.'

He looked back.

Ty pattered across the deck. 'Vander.' He stopped, panting. His eyes shone like wet pebbles. 'Vander, are we there?'

'We're close.'

Ty clambered up beside him and peered over the bulwark. He was the smallest of the lot and could barely see over. He had chosen a cloudy shirt whose sleeves drooped off his hands.

They studied the horizon. Terra Nullius's gates twinkled through pale mist. Soon, rows of shacks would coalesce along the shore and towers would soar behind.

'See those bars around the land?'

'Yes.'

'Sea gates. Every resort has them.'

Ty shielded his eyes.

'Keeps raiders out.' A shadow was spreading: a generous bay crouched behind the gates. He imagined hundreds of landies roasting beasts, beating drums and moving with music; he saw other tourists arriving from sea-stops and states, hundreds upon hundreds of well-born tourists who had not won travel tokens in lotteries but laboured and traded for them. There would be hundreds of languages, thousands of stories and an unthinkable wealth of tools. He licked his lips.

'What will we do first?' Ty asked.

'When we get there?'

'Yes.'

'We could start by flying.'

'Flying?'

'Yes.' Another itch flared across his scalp. He reached back and pinched the sweaty hair at the nape of his neck. 'Terra Nullius has a cart you can ride through the sky. It'll be as though we're flying.'

'Through the sky?'

'Yes. High over the zort on metal tracks, high enough to see everything.' A flutter touched his gut. Now that he had said it, a cart in the sky seemed ridiculous. He'd never seen any such cart at the resorts Pa had sent him to already. He hoped Gup had not made it up.

'Can we fly over the whole resort?'

'What?'

'When we go in the cart.'

'We can.'

Ty's smile was full of gaps. 'And then what?'

'Then we'll know the busiest spots to trade. You can get anything if you trade well.'

'Anything?'

'Anything.' He patted Ty's springy coils. 'But you have to look smart. Your buttons are wrong. Here.'

He bent down and worked Ty's buttons out one by one. It was a good shirt, soft with traces of ink stripes. He decided a wealthy landie had worn it before, perhaps for several years. He pushed the buttons through their proper loops. Only one button was missing and its absence was hardly noticeable.

'What will we swap?'

'Coins.' He tugged Ty's collar straight and leaned back to look at him.

'How many coins do we have?'

'We will get coins soon. We can work.'

Ty pressed his cheek against the wood. His boot nudged Evander's ankle. 'Should I get you trousers?'

Evander looked down over his tunic, over the oat smears and soup marks flaky-orange against the grey. It probably smelled but it was comfortable and he had grown so much since his last birthday trip he feared no trousers or boots in the trunk would fit.

He was almost Pa's height now, Gup had said. He just wished his arms were thicker. He touched his cheek. A beard would come through soon. It would sprout coarse and black. Then Gup would quit calling him pretty and lucky and saying he looked like Ma.

'I'll dress later. We have time.' Lantic clothes clung in cruel places. Either landies liked to be uncomfortable, so they could shuffle in their stiff way, or their bodies were cut so differently that they never felt confined. Trousers would irritate the rash on his leg. He would have told Gup about the rash but it seemed best to appear well around his birthday, in case Pa came. Pa would never take a sickly boy into his crew, not even if that boy was his lastborn son.

For all he knew, Pa could be waiting to surprise him at Terra Nullius. Giddiness tickled his calves. He could not remember the colour of Pa's beard or the distance between his eyes. Some nights he dreamed Pa had forgotten his face too, and that he had welcomed some other boy into his fleet and that was why he had not come.

'I'll get you the sparkly trousers.' Ty jumped down.

'Wait.'

Ty was already running. His shirt flared behind.

Shrieks and giggles tangled as the kids scrabbled for clothes. Ma Sahn stood in the chaos, stout as a jug and holding her hips.

The bulwark rumbled against him. That happened each time the speakers played a message. The speakers were black blocks each big as a fat man's head, held in dull cages mounted across the deck. They had been silent for days at the beginning; he had assumed them broken. Then, between mid-Lantic sea-stops, pipe music brimming with drums and chimes had erupted from their dark mesh faces. He smiled. Those songs had made his feet tap.

Static had hissed through slow days in the middle seas. Now, voices crackled.

The voices, usually male, were clearest in the quiet before dawn.

'The date is the thirty-fourth of the seventh month in year eight, UN Global Standard. You have entered private waters,' the speakers usually said. 'Identify your carrier. Trespassers will be punished.' Sometimes they chorused, 'Retreat, retreat.'

He had never heard a resort send such hostile messages, but Ma Sahn did not seem worried. Either way, they would soon find out if they were indeed trespassing.

He glanced up. The sails were bloated; they cast shadows black as bruises and within those shadows, stains from yesterday's rain stretched like pitch.

He really would miss this carrier. He stroked her trembling bulwark. She had the colours of a vessel patched together in southern seas: beams blushed purple alongside scabby ash boards. She was big, too: thrice as long as she was wide and crowded with towering masts. Her dusky flag bore no numbers, which was odd for a UN tourist ferry; instead someone had etched 'Fearless Carrier' on the news board by the captain's cabin.

Evander ducked and saw the captain's boots still rooted in the gap beneath the door.

Spray stung his neck and trickled down his back. He felt the ship groan upon a swell.

'Hai,' Ma Sahn called. She waved at him. 'Come.'

He hopped off the step and went to the trunk.

'Hurry. Come.' The smudges where rain had stung her cheeks and hands had swollen to welts. It served her well, for all the noise she had made stomping and praying through the storm. Believers weren't so bad; he just did not see why they shouted so when they claimed the Tide heard men's quietest thoughts.

'There is nothing I can't fix.' Ma Sahn plunged her arms into the trunk and dredged up a knot of sleeves. 'You'll look smart as a little landie.'

It would take more than a new shirt for that to be true. No one would think of him as little now, although he was still a boy in these seas. He had seen pictures of little landies in the pages Pa sent each year with the promise he would soon live on soil, soon attend an academy. The pictures showed children standing in rows, children with flat hair and luminous skin. They wore frilly shirts and tight trousers and boots that gleamed black.

'Evander. Choose.'

He accepted the bundle and teased a sleeve free. The cloth was coarse to touch.

'Tide help us. Look at your hair.'

He stepped back to dodge her big hands.

'Stop!' cried a gangly boy. 'They're mine.'

Ty and two other kids were locked together trying to wrest the tall boy's trousers off.

'Hai.' Ma Sahn got between them. 'Let Vander see the mirror.' She swatted and they ran squealing.

Evander's reflection confronted him with a grimace. His hair was ashy with dirt. He had caught slight colour from standing on the deck, and his moustache was coming through. He reached up and touched it. Fine hairs tickled his fingertips. He touched his nose. It looked different in this mirror: small and too pointed, like a baby bird's beak.

'The date is the thirty-fourth of the seventh month, year eight. Trespassers will be punished. Terra Nullius is private land,' intoned a speaker overhead.

'Land,' a boy piped. 'It said land.'

'Land.'

'Land.'

The chant spread.

Jekwu Anyaegbuna won the 2012 Commonwealth Short Story Prize for Africa. A fiction fellow at the Elizabeth Kostova Foundation for Creative Writing in Bulgaria, he's a recipient of the Miles Morland Foundation African Scholarship at UEA. He's been published in *Granta, Prairie Schooner, Transition,* and *The Massachusetts Review.*

Twitter: @JekwuAnyaegbuna
correnz@yahoo.com

Certificate of Infertility
An extract from a novel

I wasn't bothered that an unsmiling trainee doctor signed my certificate of infertility, although qualified doctors would show some white teeth before breaking bad news. I didn't care that I'd joined the club of men whose pumps couldn't inflate wombs. The worry about my lineage becoming extinct didn't even occur to me. What upsets me now, months later, is that my wife is pregnant, and I don't know who's responsible – a guy, a god, or a ghost.

The truth remains that lies have always been the honey and sugar of our marriage. Even before we married, I told her that a Range Rover Jeep was mine, and she cried when I returned the car to the owner after our wedding. She told me she was a fresh petal and no horny bee had perched on her, but I later met an Olympic auditorium under her skirt. Since then, I've refused to reveal to her that during the Boko Haram war a bullet speared my groin, damaging my reproductive tubes. That's why I don't shave my groin, so as to hide the scar.

Now she wants to convince me that I'm the new blood in her womb, that my fruit is functional with seeds. She smiles and rubs her hand on her bulging stomach. Women can be funny. Very, very funny.

She points at her stomach. 'Darling, this baby is going to look exactly like you,' she says, sitting on the couch.

I frown. 'How do you know?'

'You were at your best the day you ejaculated into me.'

I shake my head. What else can a retired soldier do? If a woman doesn't kill a man, nothing else can kill him.

But I'm going to unearth the source of this pregnancy today by consulting a famous witchdoctor, Baba Jesus-Mohammed, who a friend has strongly recommended. I don't have the huge money for a DNA test. And, anyway, witchdoctors have been saving our lives for ages, revealing secrets through their spiritual diagnoses, long before white men violated us with digital machines, and asked us to abandon our gods.

I'm about to leave my house to board an eight-hour bus to the village, and I have to lie again to my wife.

'Sweetie, I'm going for an official duty,' I say, my mind on my ominous suitcase hidden in a coppice of hibiscuses outside our gate.

'Go well,' she says, smiling. 'When you return, we'll agree on a name for your lookalike in my womb.'

The suitcase is full of sacrificial items: a white fowl, cowries, red candles, white sand, red cloths, a small earthenware pot, a tortoise, and duck feathers. She mustn't see these things; God, she mustn't because as far as she knows I'm a good Christian who shouldn't be caught with pagan objects.

I snort and leave.

The moving yellow bus is full of stern-looking people, men and women whose problems are engraved on their faces. From their serious looks I can tell we're all going to see the same witchdoctor. We Nigerians are restless souls. We combine charms and Jesus Christ in order to achieve anything, and we attribute the power to only Jesus Christ. Our own Jesus Christ has been credited with many unmerited accomplishments.

Our bus coughs, jerks, and picks up speed again.

I tap a man sitting to my left. Both of us are in the front seat. 'Are you sure the witchdoctor isn't a river that dries up when needed most?' I ask.

'No,' he says. 'For every problem, he knows a god that solves it.'

'And we have to pay our dues to the gods?'

'Exactly.'

'Is it right for Christians to partake in idol worship?'

He chuckles. 'Man, there's no right or wrong in this matter-o,' he says. 'Even Muslims don't trust Allah and Prophet Mohammed these days. They must visit African witchdoctors to verify things. Students patronise them, too, to make their exams easy. They hope the witchdoctors can reveal the exam questions in advance.'

'Oh, really?'

'Of course, the witchdoctors can even become invisible, sneak into the hall, and write exams for the students.'

'This is my first time going to see Baba Jesus-Mohammed,' I say.

'You won't be disappointed, trust me.'

Now we've spent seven hours and forty-five minutes on the road, but we're still going, hoping, going, almost there.

Finally, we arrive and walk to the reception desk in single file. The witchdoctor has his shrine inside a three-storey building. It seems he alone lives in this silent neighbourhood. A lady in a crumpled skirt gives each of us a number. Thank God, I'm number one.

She details the rules and regulations, 'Remove your footwear. Cut your fingernails. Items of jewellery aren't allowed inside.' She hiccups. 'Women should remove their underwear. They must be naked before the witchdoctor. I'm afraid that any woman having her period can't enter. Menstruation renders the witchdoctor powerless and blind. Any man or woman who's had sex the previous night, I'm sorry, can't see Baba Jesus-Mohammed.' She coughs. 'At the door, before you enter, you must shout your name seven times. On the stool near the door, there's a razor blade. Pick it up, cut your middle finger open, and dab the blood on the door to mark your presence.'

She hiccups again and swallows her spittle.

'Is that all, sister?' I ask.

'No, sir,' she says. 'You must submit your photo to Baba Jesus-Mohammed. Is that clear?'

'Yes, yes,' we say, nodding and glancing at one another.

None of us dares to question the rules.

It's my turn, and I perform all the drama at the door before climbing the flight of stairs. When I get into the shrine, I find Baba Jesus-Mohammed seated on the bare floor. He flashes me a spooky smile. I also feel his warm welcome through his eyes the colour of carrot juice. The Bible and the Qur'an are opened in front of him, with a statuette of a local deity which squats and stares at him. A blazing red candle stands between the holy books. There's a framed drawing of Arabic lettering on the wall, hanging alongside a big cross with moons and stars carved into the four edges. The cross carries a decaying, full-size crocodile nailed to its centre. The protruding nail looks rusty. The place smells like a loaded mortuary without electricity, and, at times, the stench of rotten fish makes its way into my nostrils. I pinch my nose. Above us, a red bulb glows, colouring a white pillow and a thick mattress in one corner. By the mattress is a pack of condoms. A black goat eats fresh grass near a bony, sad dog slurping water from the remains of a broken plastic bucket. Greasy clothes are hung on the clothesline connecting two opposite walls with peeling white paint. There's a dictionary and a calculator on a short stool near the grass-eating goat. I wonder if the animal is a journalist or a mathematician.

Baba Jesus-Mohammed wears a white gown, and faces the holy books. His head is covered with a red turban. He holds a big padlock in his left hand. The padlock could be the most potent object in the room – for locking the devil.

He asks me to offload my sacrificial items in a corner and sit before him. My tortoise crawls out, and my fowl squawks. I'm happy the animals are still alive.

'Where's your photo?'

'Here,' I say, sitting down and handing it over.

He throws it into a basket.

Baba starts chanting, 'In the name of Allah, I pray through Jesus Christ, our Lord in Heaven. Hallowed be the name of Sango, the able god of thunder and fire. I beseech the kingdom of Ogun, the iron god of ages, to come down now. Thy will be done on earth through the special powers of Ifa, the god that owns my divination.'

I notice he has one incisor missing and a gold tooth replacing another.

He holds out a needle and asks me to lean forward. Jittery blood hurries through my veins. My breathing and heartbeat quicken. I exhale loudly. He pierces my forehead, and I feel the sharp pain as blood gushes out. He asks me not to touch it. I hit my chest to show bravery. He picks up a glass cup and asks me to allow the blood to drip into it. When he's collected enough, he snaps open a bottle of schnapps and pours alcohol into the glass cup, half full. He spits into it, mixes everything with his middle finger, and holds the cup towards me.

'Drink it,' he says.

I recoil, eyeing my suitcase and the exit. 'What?'

'Drink.'

I collect the cup and sip once, grimacing as I swallow. And then I gulp down everything.

He nods, collecting the cup. 'What can I do for you?'

'I'd like to know who got my wife pregnant.'

He falls silent, shuts his eyes, and opens them again.

'Oh, it's very clear,' he says. 'Your wife isn't pregnant.'

'What?' I burst out. 'Baba, are you sure of what you're saying?'

'Jesus Christ! Don't doubt the gods. They see farther than we do.'

Has my wife lied to me again, perhaps strapping a football under her gown? She shouldn't lie about something as serious as pregnancy. Is she sick in the stomach? My mind tries to convince me this man must have impregnated her and he's here to confuse me, but I dismiss the thought.

'But, Baba—'

He holds out his hand. 'Have you paid?'

'No, Baba.'

'Allah, in that case, there's been a terrible mistake. I thought you paid the receptionist. I can't see clearly until you pay. I divine better when my stomach is full. Please drop five thousand naira into that bowl.'

He points.

I dip my hand into my pocket and pull out the money. 'Here it is, Baba,' I say, throwing it into the bowl.

He picks up the money and buries it deep in the bag sitting beside him. He sighs, then shuts his eyes, and opens them again. 'Let me ask once more. What do you want to find out?'

'Am I the one who's sent my wife on a nine-month journey?'

'Let me check.' He turns the pages of the Bible and mutters Arabic words while leafing through the Qur'an. 'Oh, the gods are having their siesta. They can't talk to me right now.' He grabs a bronze bell and rings it seven times. 'I want to wake them up, but they're all snoring.'

'Baba, that's not what I've come here to learn.'

'What do you want?'

'The truth about my wife.'

'You say she's pregnant?'

'Yes, Baba.'

'How often do you have sex with her?'

'As often as I want.'

'You must have impregnated her, *wallahi*.'

'But a doctor has said I'm sterile.'

'What?'

I spot my wife's photo among the sea of other photos stuck to the walls and cringe.

'Baba, that's my wife's photo,' I say, pointing. 'She's been here!'

'Shut up and listen to me. Man, you talk too much. Leave your wife alone and focus on your own problem. Afternoon is a wrong period to visit me because the gods can't reveal the truth at this hour of sleep. You can come back another day with more money. I recommend the morning hours. That's when the gods are getting out of bed with no sleep in their eyes. Please, go!'

The goat bleats, its voice furious. The miserable dog growls, and I know my time is up. I weep, struggling to hold back tears, as I step into the landing and run downstairs. When I get home, I'll weigh my tongue and mind, and determine what next to do.

Stephen Buoro is the 2018 recipient of the Booker Prize Foundation Scholarship. He graduated with a First Class in Pure Mathematics in 2017. In January 2019, he was awarded a UEA Humanities Studentship to study for a PhD in Creative-Critical Writing.

buorostephen@gmail.com

The 5 Sorrowful Mysteries of Andy Africa
An extract from a novel

It's just Mama and me mirrored on the TV now. She yawns, her dimples burrowing. She's almost naked, wearing only the wrapper patterned with one thousand green yellow red blocks, tied around her chest, covering her down to her knees. She yawns again. The bump fastening her wrapper loosens. She quickly opens her wrapper – I catch the dark crooked line of her cleavage, the resignation of her fallen, mitten-like breasts – straightens it and ties it again, locking it under her armpit, forming a new bump. The hem of her slip peeks. She tucks it into the wrapper. She hasn't mended her bras this weekend. She often mends her two black bras on weekends, with a needle and white or yellow thread. I don't know why she never uses black thread. Why does she want to notice the stitches?

She's finished chewing her gum. Her lips are heavy, pouty, alive, like black petals. She closes her eyes and rests her head on the sofa. Her cornrows are long and full; streaks of grey lean out of the dark mass, drooping, waving like a cornfield in the breeze as she turns and turns her head.

This is my Mama:

this is
the goddess
i want to be
and
don't want to be

this is
the seed
of my
shame

this is
the twist
of my
fear

I want to say something to her. But I don't know what to say. I feel a strange need to talk to her, a duty to hold her hand. She's so close to me. Thirty cm away. Veins pushing out to me. Breath whistling in my ear. But she feels so far away.

The older I grow, the less we seem to speak. Those yellow days when Mama and I moulded sandcastles after rainfalls... leaves smelling, stones glistening... When she laughed out loud as I tickled her sides, telling me to stop but wanting me to continue. Those speechless moments when she looked in my eyes and smiled knowingly, her dimples sucking me in... and circling round their folds, I'd find the words she couldn't speak: words without spellings, without sounds.

In times like this, in the epicentre of silences like this, I remember Ydna. And I miss him. And I try to trace the very moment when this silence began. When it appeared suddenly like mushrooms. Without a seed.

When you're younger, you're closer to the world of the Unborn, to the world of the recently Dead. Once, Ydna and I were One and The Same. We were concentric circles by day, fractals by night; he was my buddy, my shadow. This was before I turned eight. He had long, thin dreadlocks. He liked yellow shirts with blue collars, with red flowers printed on the front. I felt him everywhere, his breath tickling my skin when I slept, whistling in my ear when I played football with other kids in the neighbourhood. At night, Ydna and I whispered in the dark. We whispered after Mama and I had said Hail Mary and We Fly To Thy Patronage, after she was sure that I'd covered myself from mosquitoes with her old wrapper, that I'd closed my eyes and my chest was rising and falling normally.

Ydna and I talked about trees, the tallest one he dreamt of climbing, the sweets Okey had licked, the little homeless girl he'd seen sitting by the stream alone, with no one to talk to, her hair sandy and tousled. I shared with him my dreams of birds and my fears of snakes and juju. I was always dreaming about birds. Big, white ones. With blue eyes. Birds that neither sang nor cried. Why didn't I ever dream of sheep or lions or even snakes, but birds, arboreal birds?

Ydna always sat beside me on my mat. We inhaled and exhaled together, his head rested on his palm, his eyes on me, unblinking, my eyes opened, staring at the rain-stained ceiling, not seeing the dragon-shaped marks in the darkness, but picturing and reanimating them; his fingers and toes unmoving, his soul picking every word I said. His breath smelt of mint or leaves sweating dew; my breath smelt of eba and egusi.

Every night, Ydna and I whispered till the cocks crowed.

Everything changed when I turned eight, when I watched *The Matrix* and *Superman* and *Spider-Man* and told Ydna about them. Walls and mountains and black holes grew between us. Obstructing. Shattering. Everything changed when I told Ydna that I wanted to be like Neo. Like Clark Kent, like Peter Parker. That I wanted to be different.

That I wanted to be white.

because
only

white people

could
freeze time
could
spin in space and stop bullets
could

fly

'Ydna, only white people can fly!'

He was silent. He didn't react, as if what I said didn't mean anything. I repeated myself. Over and over. Louder and louder. A cold tear dribbling down my cheek, down my ear. Down, down until I heard the bang it made when it landed on my mat. He didn't even look away when I turned to him, when I fingered his toe. I became very sure that the mountains had grown between us because he suddenly rose and told me that he was sleepy, that he needed to go, when we hadn't even whispered for an hour.

I didn't see Ydna the next day.

Or the day after.

The rains came. Their waters smelt of fish. Looked like fish when they landed on the ground, when they rolled, when they hurried away. And at night, from my mat, through the window, I searched every drop of rain for Ydna.

My brother. His toe prodding my side. The warm, rich, spiral pain. The way his front teeth shone in the dark when he whispered, when they tore into the bread I'd saved all day for him. I kept saving bread for him even though I knew it would remain uneaten and turn to crust, by morning. But at least he still ate the freshness. My Ydna savoured the freshness.

My dreams of birds stopped.

Several months afterwards, he finally came. It was night. I was on my mat, burning with malaria. He walked into the room, dimmed the lantern so that I could see him clearer.

He just said, 'How far, Andy?' and sat down on our worn-out sofa (he'd never sat on the sofa before).

He jiggled his foot, banging the sofa with his heel, worsening my headache. I didn't mind. In fact, I got up. Shooed the malaria.

'What's up, bro?' I said.

'Fine,' he said.

'I really like your dreads. Seriously.'

'OK.'

'Did you climb that tree?'

'No.'

'Why?'

Silence.

I felt his to-fro struggle to talk to me. His eyes kept beating off the finger of my gaze. His eyes: dark, watery, rippling. In them I spotted the most complicated jigsaw I've ever seen. Each piece of the puzzle was microscopic, shapeless, and contained fish, birds, mountains, satellites, light-speed, light-years, an encyclopaedia of info.

But I was not in Them.

He leaned forward, cleared his throat, parted his big lips. Then he got up and left. And I've not seen him since.

I often want to tell Ydna that being alive isn't easy. (After all, why else did he turn back? Why did he refuse to be born?) Death and dying are easy. Even boring. Life is hard, and senseless. Life is waking up and finding hooks in your heart. If you remove any, you die. If you leave any, you die. You end up stuffing more hooks into your heart to stay alive.

But Ydna doesn't want to hear any of this. I know of his refusal to listen to me because I eavesdrop on his thoughts and record them in my diary. He accuses me of living the life he should have lived. He claims to have turned back, in Mama's womb, for a breather, so that he could refresh himself and arm his muscles for this world. But by the time he was ready, by the time he peered into Mama's womb, he saw that it was already full, nine months full. So he tried to push me back, to wherever I'd come from, so that he could slip his soul into my body and be born. But I refused to let that happen. So it was this struggle that prevented Mama from bringing me out the normal way, that made the doctors cut her belly and pull out my Cursed self. It was this struggle that made the quack surgeons cut her in the wrong places, ruin her organs, so that she's now neither a woman nor a man.

I'm sure Ydna still cares about me. This is because, since I began to think about sinking my fingers into blond hair, since I began to think of HXVX, since Zahrah Returned from the Sahara, I've felt him peeping at me a couple of times. He peeps at me through the curtains, pretending to be a light breeze so that I don't notice him. But I do. I often want to call him out on it. But I don't. I'm afraid that it would further chase him away from me. From my horizons, from my closed-bounded intervals.

About three years ago, Mama banned me from her studio. Maybe that was when it all started. That screaming silence.

Her studio is a small shop on Sharp Corner, near the main brothel of our town. Mama banned me because, one afternoon when I sat in her studio, drowsy, waiting for lunch, a ho in her twenties came to have her photo taken. She was in stilettos, a sports bra, tights, but had no knickers on. As Mama got things ready, turning on the lighting, selecting the best background, the ho walked towards me. Tapping her old iPhone, lost in thought, her pussy winking at me with each step.

'Hahaha!' she suddenly laughed. 'You dey look my vajayjay!' She turned to Mama, her laughter rising to a crescendo. 'Your boy wan fuck. He wan fuck. I go help you fuck am.'

She proposed a deal to Mama: Three shots of her and she'd give me one hour of her time. 'I get expertise to disvirgin boys o.'

Mama asked her to leave.

The ho laughed. 'Na joke I dey joke o.'

Mama insisted.

'I no dey go anywhere. Till you snap me photo.'

Mama asked her to leave and called her Satan.

The ho slapped Mama.

Mama dropped her camera beside my feet. She pushed the ho with all she had, veins jutting out of her arms, out of her neck, till she and the ho were outside, till they landed on the ground, till they rolled and rolled in the sand.

Men gathered.

The ho got up. Tore Mama's dress. Ripped Mama's bra. Mama's breasts spilled out.

two
saggy
suns

two
black
suns

The men whistled. Forcing out third eyes from the centres of their heads.

I stood. Rooted. Useless. A Semi-Man.

Mama got up. Covered herself with her sandy hands. Walked back to the studio. As she reached the doorway, the ho sprang forward and slapped her butt. Called her a prostitute. Said her butt was big enough to earn her three times what she makes from her studio.

The men laughed.

I couldn't look at her that day.

Or the day after.

Or the weeks after.

i
went
to
black

she
went
to
black

An abyss grew in my throat. I couldn't speak to her. My words kept falling and screaming as they fell. The Unspoken tapped me up at night. I gasped for air. Only found screaming silence.

I only greeted her good morning after prayer or good evening when I returned from school.

She looked at her feet when she replied with a sullen 'How are you?', not even mentioning my name. She stared at her plate when she asked me to get her drinking water, when she said thank you.

I woke up one night gasping on my cold mat. I heard a strange, croaky voice from her room. A voice weeping.

Catherine Gaffney grew up in Ireland, and obtained her BA in English Literature and Art History from Trinity College Dublin. Before focusing on her own writing, she worked in London as an editor and designer of scholarly books about art and architecture, and greatly enjoys 'shaping' narratives, both textually and visually.

caegaffney@gmail.com

Harbour Road
A short story

Brian clicks on the wiper, and watches the night.

The footpaths overflow at this hour. Crowds congeal in the fluorescent light of takeaways; women flap and teeter in spiked heels, and men sway and spurt off the steep kerb and out onto the road.

Bright threads of rain vanish in Brian's neat, clean arc. He exhales hot, white breath on his gloved knuckles, and huddles his elbows to his chest.

A sharp rap on the window, pale eyes peering in. Brian rolls it down.

'Dalkey OK?' asks the man.

Brian nods, and rouses the engine.

The man is tidy; he is young, slim and suited. He rounds the car steadily, watching for passing traffic. And though it is late – or early, depending on how Brian looks at it – the man's shirt collar is neat, and the tie, carefully tightened.

The man slides into the passenger seat and shuts the door. He breathes into his hands, and rubs his fingers in his palms.

'Whereabouts in Dalkey?' Brian asks. He taps the phone perched beside the steering wheel, and readies its GPS search bar.

'One sec.' The man pulls a phone from the pocket of his blazer, and stares at the screen. 'Harbour Road's fine, actually.'

Once they've cleared city traffic, it'll be a smooth, straight run down the coast – nice and quiet, at this time. Brian hits the indicator, and watches the queue of dark, crawling taxis. A gap emerges, and he weaves his car out onto the road. He drives slowly, braced for the loose waves of pedestrians that tumble through the yellow drift of his headlamps.

'Good night?' asks Brian.

'Not too bad,' says the man. He crosses his arms, hunches his head against the passenger window, and directs his gaze to the road.

This is a pity; Brian's eyes are itching, and conversation is helpful. He increases the volume of pulsing Europop, and, clearing city traffic, accelerates towards the suburbs.

It's one last run, and then it will be westwards, home. He will sit with his own thoughts and a cup of tea for twenty minutes in the squashy, sagging armchair, before he heads upstairs, to the warm duvet, and to Lareina. A few hours later, she will fill a flask of coffee and they will shout out and cheer from the sodden sidelines of their son's football match. He feels, on these drenched Sunday mornings, nervy and incoherent, as though he has to stitch time together. But it is worth it to see Shay fly across the soft turf, his wiry frame soloing and kicking the ball straight through the goalposts.

'You mind switching that off?' The man leans forward in his seat and grimaces, massaging his forehead with the heels of his hands.

Brian cuts the music, and slows for a set of red lights. To their left, beyond the empty railway track, is the dark bay of the city, shimmering with the bright lights that hug its curve. He slides the window down again for a hit of salty sea air, and hopes the man will not complain of the cold. Instead, Brian sees that he has parted his fingers, and is examining his taxi licence card, glued to the base of the windscreen.

The man lifts his hands away and gives a short laugh. 'Brian?'

'Hmmm?' Brian responds, prepared. The lights glow green, and he accelerates along a wide stretch of empty road that divides scruffy parkland from high stone wall.

'Are there many Brians, where you're from, Brian?'

Brian can feel the man's eyes on his cheek and he chuckles, reflexively. 'It's not so unusual.'

'It's a good name. "Brian Boru" – d'you get that a lot?'

'Battle of Clontarf,' Brian replies, in keeping with the man's jocular tone. 'My son's learning about it at school.'

'1014, 1014,' says the man, leaning back into his seat. 'Funny, the things you remember.' He points at Shay's beaming face, Sellotaped to the dashboard. 'That him, there?'

Brian nods. 'He's bigger, now.'

The roads, cast with the amber sheen of streetlamps, have begun to narrow. They ribbon past pale elegant terraces of blank windows, and Brian feels the cool air on his neck, the light drizzle.

The man slides down his own window. Over the roar of wind that whips through the car, Brian hears him humming: a repeated, fast-paced motif, a smattering of lyrics. To their left, a steep drop of pier. Brian wishes he had not skipped his last coffee break, an hour earlier.

'He plays football,' Brian says loudly, over the rush in his ears. 'He's good. He might play for Dublin.'

'That's nice,' the man yells back, before returning his attention to the dark waves through the open window, to his chopped fragments of song.

'I was never much good, myself,' shouts Brian, across the gearstick. 'At sports, I mean.'

'Yeah,' says the man. He untwists his torso and turns back to the inside of the car, his hair ruffling. He nods to the rhythm inside his own head. 'C'mere, do you know The National? They're from Ohio. I saw them in Whelan's way back, before they were big.'

'I don't know them,' Brian calls into the wind, and shakes his head, for emphasis. It's icy and refreshing on his cheeks, and he spins the wheel with ease, in line with the lightly curving roadway.

'They're good. You should listen.'

'My son,' says Brian, pointing to the photograph, 'won the schools' final. He scored three goals. And you know, we found out later, that he had broken his ankle in training, just a few weeks before.'

'Jesus,' shouts the man. 'That's deadly.'

'It's stupid!'

The man laughs, his response swallowed up by the crackling gust. Brian rolls up both of their windows, leaving an inch open in each frame.

'Why didn't you tell us what had happened?' Brian had asked his son, once they were back from the hospital. 'We would have taken you to the doctor.'

Shay raised his arms to high heaven, as though it was the most obvious thing in the world. 'Because you wouldn't have let me play!' He sighed, and relaxed against Brian's shoulder in the light of their television screen, his attention fixed on its fits of bright green AstroTurf. 'And anyway, it wasn't even that sore.'

Now, when Shay is bashed or clobbers into something on the pitch, Brian looks into his ten-year-old eyes and sees that same dismissive defiance, that insistent diminishment of pain.

'I'm fine, Dad. Really. I'm *fine*.'

The man has turned his face to the window, again. He still hums: a repeated, gravelly murmur. Brian inhales the thin rectangles of coastal air, and in the deep navy sky that curves above the water, detects the faint wash of morning.

In the summers, Lareina insists that they drive to the beach, even when the rain speckles the sand dark slate-grey. She hitches up her jeans and wades into the wash with Shay, who goes further, splashing and diving into the waves. Brian sometimes ventures in, up to his ankles, but the thick foam is a cruel, burning type of cold; it numbs his feet to dull, wayward clods.

'It's perfect, Dad!' Shay bounces from the water, waving at the shore. 'It's roasting!'

Brian laughs, shakes his legs up and down, and shudders in exaggerated disbelief.

Afterwards, they sit in the soft warmth of the car, cushioned from the wind chill, towels pressed around their sandy feet. Shay stretches across the back seat on his stomach and leafs through his books, chattering about all the countries and cities you could see across the horizon, if only you could see far enough.

'Do you think we could swim to Liverpool, if the sea wasn't so rough?'

'You'd have to be a really strong swimmer,' says Lareina.

'Do you think if I swam to Liverpool, they'd let me play for them?'

'You'd be too tired to play,' says Brian, 'with all that swimming.'

Shay flips onto his back, and stares at the grey plastic ceiling. 'Maybe I could float, for some of it. Take breaks, now and then.' He stretches one arm out from his side and strikes slowly, thoughtfully, against an imagined resistance. 'That'd be OK. Then I wouldn't be so tired. I could even play in goals for a bit, at the beginning.'

'I liked being in goals,' says Brian, 'when I was your age.'

He doesn't tell Shay that for him, the goal had been a sort of refuge. Standing between the posts, he was able to sustain a vague sense of his teammates' blurred, distant offensive, but could allow his thoughts to drift and inflate...

'Mind!' the man shrieks.

Brian brakes, and swerves to the right of two plastic wheelie bins, which are toppled, horizontally, out onto the road. He pulls in next to the steep coastal drop, and eyes the oblong obstacles through the thin horizontal lines of the rear-view window.

'That was close,' says Brian. He opens the door, and peers back. 'You wouldn't want anyone swerving left, without thinking.'

The man inhales through his teeth, and murmurs in agreement.

Outside in the air, Brian stands each bin upright, and rattles them back to the footpath. He knows that his thoughts are sagging, and takes a fresh gulp of air, but it is mixed with the stench of refuse sacks, ripped and strewn along the road. He really should have had that last coffee. He can't wait to get home, to his armchair, to his bed. Through the windscreen, he sees the man, his head lilting to one side, a frown on his face.

Brian sits back into the car, and they get moving again.

'They'll probably just blow over again,' the man says unhelpfully, after a moment.

'It'll be bright soon.' Brian hopes he sounds reasonable, rather than curt.

He is relieved to see, from the GPS, that they don't have far to go. Perhaps there'll be a garage open nearby, for something cold, sugary, caffeinated. He needs to stay awake for the long journey home. He wishes the man would stop humming. But he keeps doing it, again and again, the same tune.

'I always wanted to be in a band,' says the man, opening his window again.

'Oh.' Brian glances at the suit.

'But my dad thought law would be more sensible,' says the man, with a yawn. 'He said I had brains, so...'

'Hmm.' Brian steers the car past wrought-iron railings and high, tidy hedgerows. 'And you live around here?'

'Used to, used to.' The man lifts his pale eyes, stretches, and chuckles to himself.

'It's a very nice area,' says Brian.

The man looks out at the unfurling village, the tranquil row of flowerboxes. 'You know what, here's fine, actually.'

'Harbour Road's just around the—'

'No seriously, here's great.'

Brian pulls in beside the footpath, and glances at the red digits of the meter. 'So that's...'

'Here,' says the man. 'This should cover it.'

Brian fumbles; there are far too many golden fifties. 'Wait—'

'It's *fine*, seriously. Thanks for the lift.' The man hops out of the car, and softly closes the door. He grips the top of the open window. 'Oh, I hope your son's ankle's OK. And do listen to The National. They're great.'

'Thanks,' says Brian, clutching the wad of cash. 'Have a good one.'

The man swings his blazer over his shoulder and waves back at him through the windscreen. Brian thinks he hears him humming.

The greengrocers, the pub, the wine shop, are all silent, the awnings tightly coiled. On the footpath, a splatter of vomit. And, through a gap in the buildings, the lilting void of the sea.

Fearghal Hall is an Irish writer from Tipperary. He has a BA in Creative Writing from NUIG and is currently completing his MA in Prose Fiction at UEA.

fearghalmichaelhall@gmail.com

Quarehawks
An extract from a novel

I can see his knuckles on the sideline – four little stones, sharp and angry-white. He's the biggest umbrella in the place (massive black one we got at the Ploughin last year), but it's the knuckles that stand out. Every other hand is turned towards the far-end play. His fist is pointin at me. I can't see his face; I can well imagine the look on it though.

The sliotar is stuck around Fethard's goal when the rain comes; needles at first, then thicker and thicker until my jersey and shorts weigh a tonne, and everythin is bad-TV-signal furry. Hurleys clack and clap from the other end. I'm corner forward but prayin the ball'll stay away. No forward should want the sliotar near his own team's goal, but if it stays there, I don't have to worry about effin things up.

My marker jigs around me like a bad dance partner. He's been tryin to step on my heels since I came on. Earlier, when the ref wasn't lookin, he pure dug his studs into my ankle. It made me want to drop the hurley and run off the pitch, but the lads'd kill me.

He'd kill me.

I poke my fingers through my faceguard to scratch an itchy drop of water on my brow. The shoutin in the stands gets fierce loud, everyone's up. Yeses and Nos criss-cross and my man's in front of me – far in front, halfway-down-the-fuckin-field in front. The back of his jersey wags like a stuck-out tongue.

I start after him. My helmet rattles and bangs my throat as I go. He springs into the air and picks a white speck of sliotar from the sky. I put the head down and sprint, hopin someone nearer, someone bigger, someone else, will deal with him first. When I look up, he's right there.

Our knees and shoulders connect in a big, wet smack. He fumbles the sliotar. We both reach, but he holds me back with a leg, thumps me with his side, once, twice, three times. I slap into a pile of muck and grass. Cold sludges in the back of my helmet.

For one terrifyin moment I can't breathe. My lungs are sucked-dry water bottles.

Someone sprintin past tells me to wake up ta fuck!

When I stand, my marker's breezin through our back line, right towards the goal. He even makes a fool of Stephen Quirke. For a second it looks like he got tired or somethin because he turns away from the goal towards the sideline, but the net flinches and the umpire waves a green flag. My man curve-runs to the stand.

The noise from the Fethard supporters is unreal; you can barely hear the rain or final whistle.

All the lads fling themselves to the ground the way sulkin toddlers do. It's only a fuckin game, but honest to God some of them are cryin.

My guy really milks it and does a proper victory lap. His teammates tug-o-war him in ecstasy.

The lads tear their helmets off. Their breath streaks the air:

Fuck's sake Connor!
Where wer ya?!
We cudda drawn with em if ya'd just marked yer man.

I watch the people in the stands file out and hope ta fuck he can't hear this. My stomach tugs my bladder when I think of the ride home with him.

The Fethard boys come over to shake hands with us, but I keep hold of my hurley. I don't know who's worse, my own team for hatin me, or Fethard for makin them.

Rain pats my helmet, a pathetic there-there, while I wait for them all to leave.

In the dressin room everyone looks up like they were waitin for me. Benny the trainer asks me to take a seat so we can review.

Time for the Barney Talk.

That's what I call it, because if we ever lose they talk to us like we were part of a fuckin kids programme: All right lads, ye tried hard. They were a good team guys. They just pipped ye at the post. And my favourite, Ye gave it yer all and things just didn't go yer way. Better luck next time.

Benny says it, and Mike just nods and goes Yeah, like a back-up gospel singer.

The lads on the team, young lads, are more tuned in than these two clowns. Mikie and Benny are the supposed men we have in charge. Two fools in their forties. Their beards aren't even beards, just whiskers. The kinda lads who use their hands a lot when they talk. The lads'd only be laughin at them. And to add insult to injury, neither of them ever even played GAA. Honest to God. Not even Junior B, and any fat fool can play that. Maybe if they managed the team properly we'd've won. Maybe the rest of them will realise this and I won't get the blame.

Gerard and Stephen eye me from the corner. Gerard like a bored prince, Stephen his ogre assistant. The other lads slap their boots together and crack their socks on the bench. The air's clouded with Lynx and bad tempers.

I should've run in right after the whistle, grabbed my stuff and gone, but it seemed better to get the abuse over and done with now than in school on Monday. In front of Tracey too. Plus, I'm in no rush home.

Mike comes in, and even the way he closes the door is wimpy, touchin it back into the frame. He scratches his whiskers: Y-y-y-ye weren't too bad now lads, I-I-I-I just spoke with the Fethard manager an-an – Mike has a stutter, another reason he's annoyin – an-an-an he said well done. Ye tried hard.

Oh we did yeh, Marcus Horan snorts, fair good performances all round.

He gives three slow claps of his hands and it sets off an applause of anger:

Da fuck are you sayin Horan, and ya didn't catch a single ball all game!
Look at you and ya can't even manage a puck out.
I wouldn have ta if Connor bloody woke up!
Half-dead up there!
Says you Fox, and ya walkin round like a fuckin zombie half the game!

I squeeze the zips of my bag and soon as Mike moves away from the door I go. They're tellin the lads to remember they're a team while I slip out. Last thing I see is Gerard mouthin to Stephen and Stephen shouts Go wan! Go home! Useless!

I get halfway down the hall before the door opens:

Hold on a minute, Connor! It's Benny. I mutter about havin to leave and peg it.

The air-conditionin is on full blast, howlin through the car. I haven't changed out of my togs, and the cream leather is floor-tile cold against my legs. I belt up and watch my knees jitter. Cover them with my hands when I see him see them.

There might have been a *hmph*, but the rain bombs the windscreen so mad I can't hear. The people and cars outside are blasts of colour. He keeps the wipers on low – probably so no one'll see in.

After a minute he speaks, soft as a sigh: Fuckin disaster.

My knees jitter harder.

Were you even starting?

I can feel him lookin at me, his gaze has this hum, like a blade.

No, I – this time I hear the *hmph* – I came on at the end of the first-half, Dad.

He turns the wheel left and the veins on his hands grow; green streams between his stony knuckles.

I have a speech. It's about why I hate playin, and hate being around the lads and that I'd actually be all right if they weren't such cunts – especially Gerard. He walks around like he got the place for free. Always showin off his tan, his inverted pyramid of abs. He takes off his top and never has to worry if he'll get a jersey or not. Or if he's a spot on his back. He couldn't grow a pimple if he tried.

I chance a look over and see the tight set of Dad's jaw. He says nothin. Sometimes I think he lives by that phrase: If you don't have anythin nice to say don't say anythin at all. He's vow-of-silence quiet and I'm real mumbly so car rides aren't exactly Bant City when it's the two of us. Bein with him is like bein with the lads from school; I'm always tryin not to be noticed, and when I am it's never somethin I wanted to be seen for.

If he was playin today that Fethard lad wouldn't've gotten the goal. If he was playin we would've won handy. He'd have been captain. And he wouldn't be gettin a lift home like me, he'd be drivin his own car, girlfriend where I'm sittin. Whenever I make an eff of somethin I wonder how he would've handled it. Peelin myself from the mistake is a relief, like pickin a scab so it looks better.

Comparison is the thief of happiness – I read that online, one of those inspirational quotes no one should say out loud. I'm not goin to say it cus it makes fuck all sense anyway. How do you know somethin's any good if you've nothin to compare it to?

Rain pellets down, and even when he turns up the wipers to the last it's impossible to see out. They *wheep wheeep wheep* against the downpour. The air conditionin howls. I suction cup my ears warm and picture the other lads drivin home with their fathers and what's bein said to them. Doubt Stephen or Peter are feelin bad. They were grand. And Gerard. Even if we lose, people go on about how unreal he was. Most of em care about winnin. But they care more about playin well.

We're at Cody's Hill when a long brown smudge comes round the bend. Their car. Must be theirs cus he turns off the wipers till the rain blinds the window and they've passed. The rest of the ride is cold, and quiet and awful til the phone rings – Mum. The jumpy connection makes her even more headwreckin. She never knows when he's thick, and here she's on pesterin him with questions again.

Mum's a bit slow. Not tryin to be funny, but she is. Pure dopey sometimes. I have to go, Mum, Dad's not in the mood, he doesn't want to talk, just leave him, and even then she goes: Why? What's wrong? What is it?

She asks him where we are even though he's answered twice and starts goin: Sean, Sean! He cuts her off. When she rings back a second later, he disconnects the handset.

I can already hear them in the Sittin Room later, him tryin to watch the news, her askin who was there, who saw me make a fool of myself. That's the main reason I tell her he wants to be alone, because I'm usually the one who annoyed him, and if she finds out she makes it way worse.

Rain splatters and splatters. The wipers are on the highest settin, but it's not good enough.

LUISA HAUSLEITHNER

Luisa Hausleithner is an Austrian writer living in Norwich where she is on the Prose Fiction MA and also working as an editorial assistant for Galley Beggar Press. Besides writing, Luisa is also passionate about all things art, travelling, politics, and coffee. She is currently working on a collection of experimental short stories.

luisa.713@gmx.at

Lacuna
A short story

lacuna
NOUN
1—an unfilled space; a gap.

Is it possible to miss someone you've never met? To miss the mere idea, the illusion, the fantasy of a person who's never been alive? It must be. It's what I've been doing ever since the beginning of your non-existence.

I miss you. Every time I look at our cousin, every time I hear his laugh or see his smile, I miss you. He drops his toy caterpillar and I miss you. He reaches for my hand, his huge blue eyes staring up at me, and I miss you. He tries to eat the book I bought for his first birthday instead of reading it, and I miss you.

I try my best not to show these feelings in his presence or his mother's. I feel no resentment towards him personally, but – every time I look at him I wish it were you. And every time he looks at me he isn't. His hair is too light and his eyes are too blue. I've never seen you yet I can tell he's *not-you* just by seeing him. His entire existence is not you because he's not-you simply by existing. He's all the things you're not; all the things you wouldn't be even if you were. But you're not. Anything.

The things you're not: everything.

I lift my cup of coffee from the floor next to me and take a sip and he imitates my motion with his bottle of juice.

I miss you.

miss[1]
VERB
1—fail to hit, reach, or come into contact with.
    1.1 fail to catch.
2—fail to notice, hear, or understand.
    2.1 not be able to experience or fail to take advantage of.
    2.2 avoid; escape.

  2.3 fail to have.
3—notice the loss or absence of.
  3.1 feel regret or sadness at no longer being able to enjoy the presence of.
  3.2 feel regret or sadness at no longer being able to go to, do, or have.

'No longer' presupposes a previous presence and therefore does not apply. I, however, missed (2.1) not your presence, but: your *pre-absence*. 'Pre-,' the prefix that puts the 'pre' in 'prefix.' Literally. Your pre-absence is a state the experience of which I was denied. Now I'm left to notice the absence of (miss 3) someone who was never present.

absence
NOUN
  1.2 the non-existence or lack of.

Your absence tore a hole into our lives and left no antonym to fill it. It doesn't seem logical how someone's absence can do so much damage when there was never any presence to begin with. Your absence brought with it a lack of logic and reason and left nothing but a void of chaos. Absence. A lack of: everything.
  Everything: all the things you're not.

ab(s)-
PREFIX
1—away; from.

–ence
SUFFIX
1—forming nouns denoting a quality or an instance of it.
2—forming nouns denoting an action or its result.

Abs-ence. A noun missing (2.3) its root. The nominalisation of a prefix through its suffix. *Away-ing.* Your away-ing is the only memory I have of you and it, by definition, does not exist; and this non-memory is the only thing I have to cling to and it is *no-thing.*

exist
VERB
1—have objective reality or being.

e(x)-
PREFIX
1—out.
2—upward.
3—thoroughly.
4—denoting removal or release.
5—forming nouns which denote a former state.

And his objective reality reminds me constantly of the *ex-istence* of your abs-ence and your ex-possible-maybe-someday existence and I miss you.

mis-
PREFIX
1—wrongly.
   1.1 badly.
   1.2 unsuitably.

And your abs-ence, really, is a *mis-abs-ence* because it is so wrong and you're doing it so badly and it isn't suitable at all. And I hate that your mis-abs-ence prevents me from enjoying (VERB 1 take delight or pleasure in) his presence. And I hate that I can no longer look at a prefix without imagining its abs-ence and that I can no longer look at my cousin without thinking of yours. And I hate the fact that he is present and you're not. And I hate that I can think these thoughts while he is here, looking up at me with his blue eyes that are so wrong – his *mis-eyes* – and he is smiling at me and I hate that I cannot smile back because I am thinking of prefixes and –

I notice too late that his foot's come dangerously close to my coffee cup. Before I can stop it the last of my drink is spilled on the floor. Fail to catch (miss 1.1). His mis-eyes – blue; wrong – go wide as he watches how the coffee spreads across the wooden floorboards. I bite down my anger and wipe up the drink with my sock. I have no reason to be angry, I know. It was my fault not to pay attention and yet I can't help thinking that if it were you and not him my coffee would not have spilled. Only you're not. Anything. You're no-thing. There is no you and there never was. Pre-absence is the closest you've ever been to existence. Only you haven't. Been. Anything. You haven't been. That's the point, which I keep missing (2). There has been no you. And *no-you* is the closest you'll ever be to being.

miscarriage
NOUN
1—the spontaneous or unplanned expulsion of a foetus from the womb before it is able to survive independently.
2—an unsuccessful outcome of something planned.

It's right here in the dictionary; right between misappropriate and miscast. Just another word; black on white, Calibri, 10pt, maybe.

expulsion
NOUN
1.2 the action of forcing something out of the body.

Something. Expulsion of a foetus. Something. They don't mention what goes along with this expulsion. No 10pt word is wasted on the *expel-ence*. No mention of the tears, the screaming, the pain. No mention of the swollen eyes, the sleepless nights, the abs-ence following the pre-presence turned never-existence, the possible-maybe-someday-you turned no-you, the no-thing turned lack-of-some-thing.

carriage
NOUN
1—any of the separate sections of a train that carry passengers.
2—the conveying of goods or passengers from one place to another.
3—a person's bearing or deportment.

Wrong transit. Bad delivery. Unsuitable posture. Maybe if we used these terms instead, then your abs-ence wouldn't be off limits (PHRASE 1.1 not to be mentioned or discussed.). Maybe if we talked in synonyms your non-presence wouldn't have to be abs-ent from our conversations.
   Mama, do you still feel sadness at no longer being able to enjoy (miss 3.1) *his possible maybe-someday existence? Mama, do you lie awake at night sometimes recalling the* unsuccessful outcome*? Mama, do you also have to resort to dictionaries in hopes of defining the* away-ing *and to avoid talking about trains?*
   Your non-existence is a weight hanging over every conversation. Every mention of as much as a 'wrong' or a 'train' becomes Damocles' sword in the light of your non-presence. I never knew that no-thing could be this heavy. Your abs-ence is ubiquitous (ADJECTIVE 1 present, appearing, or

found everywhere). And yet no other topic is as forcefully avoided (miss 2.2). I hate that I can't tell my mother how sorry I am and that your father still doesn't have anyone calling him *Dad* and I hate that it's my fault for not doing anything about these things and instead I blame your abs-ence because your presence would have taken this weight off my shoulders but now it won't. You won't. Because you're not. Anything. And I hate that your father has never been more than a stepfather and I have never been more than an only child and there was only ever so much as the possible-maybe-someday-chance of something more and I'm sorry.

only
ADVERB
1—and no one or nothing more besides; solely
2—no longer ago than
3—with the negative or unfortunate result that.

ADJECTIVE
1—alone of its kind, single or solitary.

CONJUNCTION
1—except that; but.

I am only an only child and your father is only a stepfather and our mother is only my mother and you are only the fantasy of a possible maybe-someday-existence, only for that ex-istence to be spontaneously ex-pelled from the womb. Only you are so much more than that.

sibling
NOUN
1—each of two or more children having one or both parents in common; a brother or sister.

sister
NOUN
1—a woman or girl in relation to other daughters and sons of her parents.

Or you could have been. Should have. You should have been a daughter or a son and I could have been a sister (1) and we would have been siblings (1) only we're not. Siblings. I'm not a. Sister. You're not. Anything. You were planned and wanted and wished for and I was an accident and you're only a possible maybe-someday-existence and I'm only an only child and you're gone and I'm here and I –

I don't want to carry this burden of never-siblings on my shoulders every day. This weight of no-you and your mis-abs-ence and everything you've never been. Everything you'll never be. I didn't ask to live in your stead and I don't know how I'm supposed to make up for this life not lived and I know you would have been so much better at it than me. At living. At being a daughter or a son or an only child and at loving our parents equally because they would have been your parents equally. Only they're not. Because you're not. Anything. And I know you would have held them together where I have been nothing but another wedge to drive them apart because 'she's not even your daughter' would not have been a valid argument anymore and I miss you.

He is holding my empty cup of coffee as if he'd been born to do so, lifting it to his mouth and biting into the ceramic. I take it from his hands before he drops it. He smiles at me and his mis-eyes don't show any resentment towards me for taking away his toy and I wonder what my eyes might show and I remember the day I first heard about his soon-to-be existence and I miss you.

I hadn't even been told about the possible-maybe-someday-you until after it had turned no-you and yet I couldn't stop my mind from making up scenarios of what life would be like without the *bad conveyance*; what no-you would be like.

Would you have brown eyes like our mother and me? Or would your eyes be blue, like those with which he's looking up at me now, wondering or not wondering, but making me wonder about his maybe-wondering whether I despise him?

Would you have our knobbly nose? Or your father's long fingers? Our thick hair and tendency to be short sighted? Or his clumsiness and habit of falling asleep before the film is over? Our obsession with coffee? Or his addiction to caffeine? Would you have our harsh sense of justice or his placid disposition? Our at times annoying need for logically correct argumentation or his ridiculous sense of humour?

Neither. You won't be anything because you are no-you and your non-presence and your *never-inheriting-any-of-these* temporarily disrupted both our sense of justice and your father's sense of humour. Your going from pre-existence to abs-ence has removed all logic from our mother's argumentation and all peacefulness from your father's temper. The turning from possible-maybe-someday-you to no-you turned his humours from sanguine to choleric and all that was left was arguments and anger, and tears and shouting, and trained repression on pained expressions and

    your abs-ence
      ubiquitous

Amber Higgins is a Canadian fiction writer and poet whose work has been published in *Existere Magazine*, *Tinderbox Poetry Journal*, and others. Her story, 'Little Moon', was shortlisted for the 2016–17 Galley Beggar Press Short Story Prize. She holds a BFA in Writing from the University of Victoria, and was the recipient of the International Excellence Scholarship at UEA.

amberhiggins@live.ca

Lie
A short story

The wool is dark and rough, the type of grey you'd avoid sailing on, were it an ocean and not a blanket. Joan Theodora Bernardo is accustomed to its itchy weight. On a typical morning, she is reluctant to get up for work. But she feels the cold in her teeth, and knows before opening her eyes that the sodden brown drawl of autumn has lifted.

She climbs out of bed and shuffles across the carpet to the small window. On the other side, centred within the pane, is a spider's web, so hairy with frost that it looks too heavy for its anchors. In the garden, the rhododendrons are frosted, too, and between their branches, the lawn shines white. It's been a few years since the last proper winter, and she's looking forward to her walk to work – the slap of air on her cheeks, and the way the grassy boulevards will crackle beneath her footsteps.

The dresser holds a collection of thermal underwear that belonged to her father. Joan selects one with a shot waistband, better to accommodate the fullness of her hips. She pulls on her black work jeans and a turtleneck. His Cowichan sweater hangs from a hook on the back of the bedroom door. She slips it on. Like the blanket, the wool is weighty and scratches her skin, but the fit is perfect, as her build is much the same as his was: squat, with a round tummy; square shoulders and strong arms.

At the foot of the bed, the boots: old black leather, with hook eyelets from shin to crown, and scuffed toe boxes. They do not have steel caps; her father was too tough for such things. She pulls them on and makes her way to the bathroom, where the sink is cracked yellow, and the toilet lid is covered with pale green carpet.

She lifts the lid and sits down. The seat is very cold, which calls to mind the warmth of it each morning after he had been there – often for over an hour – with his cigarettes, mug of coffee, and plans strewn at his feet. She can still smell the tobacco, even though it's been two years since a match was struck in this room.

In the upper right corner of the mirror, rot has formed dark lacework on the glass, and when she stands just so, it looks like a headpiece has been pinned to her reflection. She sees his features in her own: the thin lips, wide, pulpy nose, watery blue eyes. Her father in a black crinoline fascinator hat – an image that would've horrified him. This makes her laugh, but the sound – too loud and singular – rings strange against the walls. She splashes water on her face, and pats down her curls. When did the grey overtake the black?

Joan decides against eating her usual oatmeal at home. If she leaves now, there will be time to stop for something – perhaps a bran muffin – at the new coffee shop by the four-way. And maybe she'll even take a stroll through the woods across from Pearl's Grocer.

She dons her father's mitts and toque. When she opens the door, a sharp wind swipes a painting from the wall: the celestial-eyed leopard on black velvet. The one – she imagines – he watches through. Joan moves to hang it back up, but stops when she hears a familiar voice coming from the yard. Measured. Tinder-dry. She'd recognise it anywhere. Even after all these years.

Randy Buckam is standing on the front lawn with a woman. He looks much the same: eyes huge and dark behind spectacles; small mouth and chin; lean-limbed, even in winter garb. The woman is tall – at least a head taller than him – and wears a long racing-green coat.

As Joan moves closer, she sees that his cheeks have sagged a little. His hairline has retreated, and what's left is brushed with grey.

'Jesus H Christ it's you. Joan Theodora Bernardo.'

Randy welcomes her into a hug and even through their layers she can feel the tremble between them.

'What are you doing here?' she asks.

'I didn't see a car in the drive. And, well, I've just been showing Dizz – my wife – the old neighbourhood. Love, this is Joan.'

Joan feels Dizz clasp her hands within her own. They are large and somehow warm, and her fingernails are lacquered orange. Joan is aware of her own plainness.

'I remember the name,' says Dizz. 'Didn't your dad punch poor Randy straight into the garden after catching you two kissing on the sofa?'

Joan's neck flushes in spite of the cold as she remembers the couch and the two of them – just seventeen – drunk on lemon gin. His fingers inside her, marks in her vision like water hemlock blooms. Explosive umbels of white. And then, how the door swung open and cracked against the wall. Her father, pulling at his own hair, then at Randy's shirt. The black switch gone off in his eyes.

After forty years it should be funny. Joan wishes someone would laugh. She tries, but gasps instead.

Dizz's fingers are now wrapped tight around Joan's wrists, but her expression is soft, not unkind. Her head is so large it strikes a mythical note. Her features, too: kestrel nose, thick eyebrows, and eyes winged with white pencil. Her hair, dyed copper, is slicked to her scalp. It is difficult to place her age. At last, she releases Joan's wrists.

Randy looks towards the house as he speaks: 'So, your dad. Is he...'

'Gone,' says Joan. 'Two years now. And your mother?'

'Deteriorating. That's why we're here, actually. She has dementia. Refuses to eat. I'm sorry about your dad.'

'I'm sorry about Winnie.'

'She keeps escaping the care home in the middle of the night. They find her just off Dallas Road, knee-deep in the ocean in her nightdress. A couple weeks ago she soiled her underwear and threw them out the window of her room. The poor caretaker found them in the garden.'

'She did what?' says Dizz. 'I didn't know that.'

'Yes. I told you.'

'I don't think you did. I would've remembered.'

'You were on the computer. Researching mallow plants or something.'

'Regardless,' says Dizz. 'If I end up like her just fucking shoot me.'

Randy looks up at the frosted branches of the Douglas fir and chews on his bottom lip.

Joan wouldn't mind getting dementia. She imagines herself up to her waist in the dark ocean, her lucidity receding with the tide. But instead of a nightgown, she's dressed in her father's clothes.

'Mallow-pink ice cream,' says Dizz. 'I remember now. You know better than to tell me important things while I'm doing research.'

Randy removes his spectacles and digs his palms into his eyes. 'Dizz runs a boutique ice cream shop in London with our son, Shale.'

'And I'm over the stars excited about our spring specials. Gorse Blossom and Nettle Tea. Hand foraged from the countryside by Shale. Don't they sound divine?'

Randy shakes his head. 'If I remember correctly, Joan prefers plain old chocolate.'

He looks to Joan with an intensity that is meant just for her. A sort of stile that allows only the two of them access to the memory. She knows he is thinking of their spot, and the day he told her over milkshakes that he was headed overseas.

'Mr Mike's shut down,' she says. 'A few years ago, now.'

'Oh, that's a shame,' says Randy. 'The town though. It really hasn't changed much. I saw Wendy Lansdowne at the Petro-Can. Did you know she married Dale Thomson?'

Joan nods. They swing cheerily through her till every Saturday and spend around four hundred dollars on prime cuts of meat, macadamia nuts, and full-fat dairy. They're on a ketogenic diet. He is doing it to help his diabetes. She is doing it to lose weight, because she's having an affair.

'Did Wendy tell you about their diet?' says Joan.

Randy begins to laugh and for a moment it warms her to see his gummy smile. Until she remembers him flat out on the lawn, mouth open, the dark swell of blood. Her father's hands going back for more.

'I can't believe you're still here,' says Randy. 'In this house.'

'I couldn't do it,' says Dizz. 'We've moved, oh, at least a dozen times over the past ten years. I love moving. Changing furniture and paint colour. I'd feel stagnant otherwise.'

'It's exhausting,' says Randy. 'I'd be happy to never move again.'

Joan is breathless. Words that she didn't hold before now have gathered on her tongue like spit and she knows they will come out easily.

'I don't live here. I've got a great apartment downtown and I'm dating. Her name is Karolina. I just came to organise some things. The house. I'm putting it on the market come spring.'

All around, the branches have begun to drip. By now, she must be quite late for work.

'Our daughter Violet is a lesbian,' says Dizz. 'She's doing her PhD at London Met. We're very proud of her.'

Randy opens his mouth and then closes it again. He reaches out to touch Joan's elbow, pulls back. 'I had no idea. That's wonderful.'

He takes out his cellphone and for a moment Joan thinks he might ask for her number. Then, he returns it to his jacket pocket.

'What time are we meeting with Winnie's caretaker?' says Dizz.

'In about an hour.'

'Right. We should be off, then. Really lovely to meet you.'

And then, Dizz bends down and kisses Joan on the edge of her mouth. Her breath smells of sweet liqueur. Peaches. Joan looks to Randy, to see if he noticed the gesture, but his gaze is turned towards the house.

She could continue down the fir-lined street, three blocks, through the double doors of Pearl's Grocer, along the dairy aisle to the locker room and hang her things in number thirty-three; don her green apron and plastic name tag and blot sweat from her face with toilet paper; carry on past the deli, with Carol Flemming behind the counter, skin soft as an apricot, always in a new shade of lipstick, looking dignified in spite of the fluorescent bulbs, the hairnet, her gloved hands, one holding a ham, or peppered salami, the other, waving; down the ethnic aisle to her till, with ancient Mitsy Rogers on her left, and young Andrew Collins on her right; hello, how are you, fine, fine, sorry I'm late; count her float then welcome familiar faces through; enter codes for Bartlett pears and pine nuts; scan goat's cheese and Manuka honey.

At the day's end, she could shuffle home in the dark. Pause in the door to her father's shop and taste the sharpness of altered metals. Here's the leather apron on its hook. Here's the bench, with its chisels, gouges, punches and rasps. The slack tubs filled with oil and brine; their still, veined surfaces. She could hang the painting back on the wall. Boil water for tea in the cast-iron kettle made by his hands and sit on the velvet purple couch and try not to think of bitumen-black eyes and how things could've been different.

Instead, she walks east through town. There are few cars. The ice on the sidewalks has melted and reflects the sky. A new father pushes a stroller; its wheels cut through the shimmer of blue.

She thinks of Winnie; the dark waves sucking at the hem of her nightgown. How it would feel to stand there, just for a little while, in the simplicity of the cold.

A young man sits cross-legged on the boulevard in front of the Shell gas station. He's plucked the skin from his bare arms and holds a cardboard sign: *spare change for food.* For a moment, Joan considers giving him her woollies. She raises a mitted hand to her toque. His eyes flash, expectant. Then he coughs, severing the impetus.

She flushes and mumbles an apology. Continues towards the Pacific Ocean, already anticipating the icy lick and pull as the water floods then rises above the top of her father's boots.

KHURAM HUSSAIN

Khuram Hussain is a British-Pakistani writer with over ten years of experience working in technology, venture capital and investment banking. He is interested in writing which explores themes of social alienation, isolation and self-image, related to the unintended consequences of technology and social media.

khuramhussain@gmail.com

Bright Endings
An extract from a novel

It all begins here. He stands at the entrance of BA's First Wing at Heathrow Terminal 5 with one person in line ahead of him. Usually there are none. Usually there is a free counter for him to check in the moment he arrives, after a routine journey from his apartment in Old Street via the Hammersmith line, Paddington, and the Heathrow Express, to the airport, which takes sixty-seven minutes. Today the terminal is busy. There is still one person in line ahead of him, a man who appears to be his age, thumbing his phone as he taps a disjointed rhythm on the floor with his Flyknit sneakers. He notices the man's grey shell carry-on. The Under Armour sweatpants the man is wearing are the same style as his, but blue instead of black. His loose white T-shirt and black Ray-Bans project an air of cool, the fatally relaxed look of someone off to a resort: St Lucia, maybe, or Palm Springs. He wonders if this man, too, quit his job last week.

The attendant at the entrance signals for the man to proceed. A moment later it's his turn, and he hurries past a bouquet of tulips to one of the ten counters. A uniformed employee asks for his passport, then his place of destination, and he tells her. She asks if he has a visa for South Africa, and he says he does. She projects the mannered, overly polite persona people in England often adopt, not from some natural, cheerful sense of sociability but as an expression of their own civilised detachment. When the woman inquires if he has bags to check, he places his suitcase on the scale. Normally, he has no bags to check. He hates checking bags and takes great pains to travel only with his carry-on, assailed otherwise by a bout of impatience, an agitation that inhabits him every time he is detained at his destination awaiting the slow-motion march of his luggage. But today he has no choice but to travel with luggage, today he has his oversized Tumi suitcase with him.

Thank you, Mr Hussain, the woman says and returns his passport interleaved with his boarding pass; he cringes. He hates it when people call him by his last name. He believes it implies a level of formality grounded in some artificial social hierarchy. He hates hierarchies. Also, being called

Mister makes him feel old. He doesn't think he's old. Just thirty-five. And four months. He's been counting, aware that he still has a few years ahead of him before he officially goes through his midlife crises.

He walks past the sparkling chandelier wall to the private security lane and scans his boarding pass. He picks up a tray, deposits his hand luggage, turns, and whisks through the body scanner. None of the security personnel gives him a second glance, nor feels obliged to administer any special pat-downs, to fish through his pockets, to fondle his genitals, even though he is a brown-skinned male with a last name that flags him for 'random' security checks every time he boards a flight to America. As he waits for his bag, he wonders if the busybodies at security will treat him with such benevolence in the economy channel. Truth is he doesn't know. He has yet to pass through the economy section since moving to London for work and has two more years to enjoy his Gold Card privileges, having accrued enough Tier points to defer the significance of the moment.

He collects his bag, walks straight through a snug, well-lit hollow into the first-class lounge. A sweet floral smell penetrates the room. He takes in the room's earth-toned fixtures, the chandeliers, the potbellied espresso machines, the red-rimmed crystal goblets at the bar where champagne bottles gleam. Below the flat screen is a shelf with an assortment of newspapers and magazines arranged in neat piles, and he takes one from each, simply because they are available for free. A story on Brexit features on the front page of the *Financial Times*. He eschews the publication in favor of *The Sun* and *Daily Mail*, with headlines like 'Obesity Britain,' '1 in 5 Brit Muslims' Sympathy for Jihadis' – so rousing. He has no interest in the political events shaping the country. This is also true for the politics of other countries, although he'd think twice before making such a confession in public; he has spent the last six years working with crusading valour to pressure governments to be more transparent and accountable to their citizens. That is what brought him to the UK from America. And that is where he now lives as a proud, permanent resident after passing his Life in the UK Test a year ago, faithfully committing to memory the values and principles that govern British society – democracy, individual liberty, and tolerance – along with the dates of famous battles, the height of important landmarks, and other indispensable nuggets of knowledge, like the fact that Sake Dean Mahomed brought curry to the UK when he opened the Hindoostane Coffee House on George Street, London, in 1810.

He finds a seat close to the business centre where it is quieter. He knows the lounge intimately. He has been on more business trips than he could ever have imagined or wanted. He cuts past the two gilt-edged black horse sculptures at the other entrance and strides to the buffet. There's a dinner spread with salad, cheeses, pasta and a Thai curry. Labels mark each item with allergen information indicating whether it is suitable for vegetarians or gluten free. Waiters of South Asian descent bustle in and out the kitchen clearing plates, replenishing the buffet, weaving noiselessly through tables of white patrons. In another life he can see himself working here. In this one too, if the writing thing doesn't work out. He laughs at his own joke, forks some salad on his plate, some protein, and pours himself a glass of water (he avoids alcohol when flying). He makes sure never to drink before a flight, or during one, ever since he broke up with J. He retraces his steps to his seat. A woman in a nautical striped outfit sits fanning herself with a fashion magazine, feet up on a padded stool. A narrow strip of the runway stretches behind her through the floor-to-ceiling window, the sky suffused with a faint dusky blush, like a purple bruise.

The flight to Cape Town is on time. He has twenty minutes before the plane starts boarding, plenty of time to relax, he thinks as he registers the flight information. He fishes out his laptop from his bag and connects to the Wi-Fi, taking a gulp of his water, jittery with anxiety for other reasons. He has never flown to Cape Town in economy class. Nerves almost make him choke up his food. A terror seizes him as he thinks about crying babies, about spending eleven hours and thirty-five minutes on an airplane in the absence of a flat bed. This, for some reason, is followed by the realisation he will not have sex for an entire month – the amount of time he expects to be away. This has little to do with Cape Town itself, which is the most gay-friendly city on the African continent, a kind of second home to him, given its proximity to Johannesburg where he has travelled for work countless times. It is because he's planning to spend the month writing, trying to finish the novel which has consumed the last five years of his life. The book for which he left his job. And lost a relationship. And several friends, people with whom he has lost contact over the years, trapped in the spiral of his own thoughts, a vortex of confused ideas and erratic impressions and diabolic fixations, a kind of mental fortress from which he has found it impossible to escape.

A notification pops up on his phone saying his flight is ready to board. He checks the time, lingering. It will take him, at most, fifteen minutes to get to Gate C63, even if he has to wait for a connecting train, and with almost an hour before departure, he has plenty of time. He wants to escape the crowds for as long as he can. He nibbles on his salad; he realises he has taken more than he can eat, that he's not that hungry and sets his plate aside. He wonders whether the curry is any good and walks back to the buffet, loading up another plate. When he walks back, he starts to skim a section of his novel, the opening which he has been reworking over the last few days. He reads the first paragraph. It reads like shit. Like most of his work. He has no confidence in his ability to write. But there are books in the market that are worse than his. They're sitting on the bestseller lists. That helps him keep going. Every day.

He snaps his laptop shut, checks the time, and opens Grindr. He spends the next few minutes talking to other men, but only the ones within a hundred feet of his radius. He sits there for some time, fighting against the weight of his desire and his boredom, immersed in a world in which he finds it easy to lose himself, to lose restraint – a world in which the effort of regaining his connection to reality defeats the whole purpose of the experience. Ten minutes later he's still talking to these men. He yawns, checks the time. He gets up, realising he needs to leave now or he will miss his flight. That has never happened before, but it could happen today within the scope of a world of firsts, the line at the check-in, being homeless, the silence of his inbox, like the closing in of a menace from all sides.

He packs his computer, and walks. A man brushes past him, turns, fixes him a look before he enters the disabled toilet.

He stops, turns, follows him in.

He sits in the plane, feeling a bit blah. People are scampering through the aisle beside him and he's on his phone scrolling through his Instagram, suspended in a zone of oblivion between action and fulfilment. Images of shirtless men flicker on his feed and the light of the dusk recedes broken through the window to his side as he waits for the plane to take off, drained of any degree of introspection. Remorse is an emotion that is lost on him. Over time he has learned to rationalise his perilous encounters. Promiscuity is the absence of romantic stability, a by-product of his independence, an inevitable satisfaction of the vagabond's hunger, he likes to tell himself. These encounters provide him with a sense of human connection, as transient as it may be. They thrill, they excite, break the rhythm of a mundane urban existence, while masking his longing for love, a longing which is infinite and which, he suspects, no one person can satisfy. In a way, he's realised, he's not that different from J.

Matt Jones wrote the book for the musical *Leave to Remain* (Lyric Theatre, Hammersmith: 2019). 'Theatre at its magnetic best' – *Evening Standard*. In 2019, Matt wrote two episodes of Abi Morgan's *The Split*. He has written over twenty episodes of broadcast television, including *Doctor Who*, *Torchwood* and *Mr Selfridge*.

matt.jones@hotmail.co.uk

The Scandal of the Street
An extract from a novel

Marcus was fourteen the night the scandal broke, watching *Top of the Pops* with his sister. His dad was in his armchair, pretending to read *The Leicester Mercury*, but staring at the pretty, heavily made-up singer of a new band that had claimed the number one spot. His father had a glazed look in his eyes and a wet smile curling at the edge of his mouth.

'Er, Dad,' Mel said, 'could you put your tongue back in your mouth?'

'I can look,' their father replied, flushing with embarrassment. 'What? She's a good-looking girl.'

Mel turned to her brother and gave him a knowing look. Marcus felt his insides tighten. This wasn't good.

'You fancy her?' Mel asked their father.

'I'm not so very old, you know.'

Mel was enjoying herself now. 'Dad, that's a bloke.'

'What?'

'*Boy* George. You fancy a man.'

Marcus's dad looked again at the small, faux wood panel TV, where George O'Dowd, in braids and flowing robes, was swaying to the lilting reggae beat.

'Well, what's he dressed up like that for? It's bloody ridiculous.' His father's Welsh accent stirring, as it always did when he became angry.

Mel was giddy with laughter now and Marcus joined in enthusiastically, fearing not to might somehow incriminate him. His mother came in from the kitchen, alerted by their father's tone.

Marcus turned to his mum, a big forced grin on his face. 'Dad fancies a man! You married a poof!'

'Well, you'd know all about that!' his father snapped.

Silence. The room became still. Marcus couldn't look at anyone. All he could hear was his heartbeat thumping in his chest. He stared at the paisley whirls in the carpet and the deep burn where he'd once lit a sparkler after his sister had told him it was an indoor firework. He became aware that his mother was talking to him.

'Marcus, go up to your room,' she said, quietly.

Marcus left, his eyes fixed on the floor. His mother and father stood motionless behind him, waiting for him to leave before they spoke. Even his sister was still and silent. Marcus moved on autopilot. Like a ZX81 overheating, his thoughts had crashed. His mind refused to compute what his father had just accused him of. From the sanctity of his bedroom, he heard fragments of his parents' argument.

'... you mollycoddle him...'

'... he's sensitive...'

Marcus felt his cheeks warm with shame. The argument ended abruptly. Marcus heard the front door slam beneath him. He moved to the window and saw his father marching across the front drive with Barney on a tight lead. The dog scampered to keep up, oblivious to his owner's mood. His father glanced back towards the house. Marcus ducked down below the window for a moment, fearing his father's gaze.

There was no pleasing his father. Marcus had tried. It had been easier when he was younger. At ten, it had been enough to ask his father if he could have a *Football '78* stickers album. Marcus hadn't had any interest in the stickers, but he knew his father wanted him to want them. When he'd asked for them, his father had ushered Marcus quickly out of the house, perhaps fearing he might change his mind, and driven them down to the local newsagent in their grumbling Renault. His father had taken the sticker book proudly to the counter, as if they were embarked on some tribal initiation to manhood.

'I'll take this,' Marcus's father had said, a little too loudly, 'and a pack of the stickers.'

'Thanks Dad!' Marcus had exclaimed, feigning enthusiasm. His father had looked down at him, perhaps for the first time feeling as if he could make sense of the son he routinely caught enacting intricate soap operas with borrowed Sindy dolls.

'Make it two packs,' he'd added, and ruffled Marcus's hair.

On the way home, Marcus had been allowed to sit in the passenger seat of the car. He'd torn open the packets. The names of the teams on the cards – *Motherwell, West Bromich, Ayr United* – as alien to him as the faces of the players, with their long, unkempt hair, confident smiles and thick moustaches. His father's face was partly obscured by the bushy beard he'd been cultivating, much to Marcus's mother's irritation. It curled around the crumpled collar of the musty army jacket he habitually wore on his social work visits. The jacket smelt of garages and the underside of cars.

And like the footballers on the sticker cards, it belonged to a world which Marcus knew, even at that age, he could never hope to belong.

Across the street, Marcus watched Andrew Garner mowing his parents' lawn. Andrew was three years older than Marcus. He had a mop of dirty blond hair, wore a black CND T-shirt which clung to his skinny frame and had a quiet confidence which made grown-ups uneasy. Marcus's family had holidayed with the Garners for as long as he could remember. His mother and Angela Garner were best friends, always in and out of each other's kitchens. One of Marcus's earliest memories was standing in a paddling pool in the Garners' back garden, watching Andrew and a school friend having a water fight, naked. As they chased each other around the garden, firing streams of water at each other from old washing-up liquid bottles, Marcus had been transfixed by Andrew's body, the water shining on his skin.

There was a knock at his door, startling Marcus out of his reverie. He knew it was his mother. His sister never bothered knocking and he couldn't remember his father ever coming into his room. He turned away from the window and sat down on his bed as his mother came in.

'I brought you a Creme Egg,' she said, hovering by the door. He didn't reply, so she crossed the room and put it in his hand. Marcus hoped she'd leave without talking about what had just happened downstairs. No such luck.

'Your father's... Well, your father's just your father.'

Marcus focused on peeling the brightly-coloured foil from around the chocolate egg.

'We love you, you know that, right?' she said. For a moment they sat in silence. Finally, she kissed him on the forehead and left the room. He watched her disappear downstairs.

Alone, Marcus bit into the chocolate shell of the egg. The soft gooey contents stuck to the back of his teeth. He scraped it off with his tongue, taking some comfort in the sugar which slid slowly down his throat.

When he was ten, Marcus and Colin, Andrew's younger brother, used to creep up to the golf course beyond the school fields and steal golf balls. They'd bring them back to Marcus's father's garage and smash them open with a hammer. Inside they found another ball made of rubber netting. And when they ripped that open, at the heart of the golf ball was a greeny-brown goo. Marcus remembered thinking that if you ripped him open, at the heart of him, you'd find the same repellent awfulness.

He swallowed down the last slick of sugary yolk as he dug out his Sony Walkman. He slid in a Joan Armatrading cassette, put the orange foam headphones over his ears and turned it up loud. He had just started listening to side two when his sister burst into his room, her face pale and furious. She shouted something at him he couldn't hear over the sound of the music.

'What?' he said loudly, and pulled off his headphones.

'We're getting out of here!'

'I'm not going anywhere with you.'

Andrew Garner appeared behind her. He was still sweaty from mowing his parents' lawn. He pulled up his CND T-shirt and wiped his face with it. Marcus couldn't resist risking a glimpse of Andrew's bare stomach and skinny abs. Andrew was only seventeen, but he already had a line of hair from his belly button down to the waistband of his jeans. Marcus sucked on his lower lip and looked away. Andrew hadn't been in Marcus's bedroom for years. Marcus was suddenly aware of the boxes of battered games stacked on top of the wardrobe, and the Airfix Millennium Falcon which hung from the ceiling on fishing wire.

'Is he coming?' Andrew asked Mel.

'I suppose I'm not doing anything.'

Marcus was surprised to see Colin coming up the stairs behind them, out of breath and a little sweaty. Colin was in Marcus's year at the local comprehensive, but despite having been friends at primary school, they never acknowledged each other there. Colin was forever wheezing from his asthma, and proudly claimed that on one occasion it had almost killed him.

'What's going on?' Marcus asked. 'Where are we going?'

On the bus into town, Marcus sat next to Colin. Andrew and Mel sat together on the seat in front of them. Marcus's sister didn't speak. She just stared out of the window and looked as if she might burst into tears at any moment. Marcus asked them both what had happened but neither of them replied. Colin looked at Marcus and shrugged. He didn't know either.

Mel took them to a reggae concert which their parents had explicitly forbidden her to attend. An act of rebellion which was completely out of character. His sister never did anything wrong. Marcus had always thought she was incapable of it. The concert was in a rundown community centre in Highfields, a district made up of red-brick terraced houses which had been written about in incendiary terms in the local paper after violent police protests the previous summer. Little kids were playing outside, circling each other on tricycles and kicking balls around the dusty scrubland.

The community centre had rounded metal cages over its windows, which reminded Marcus of the bug eyes of insects. As he entered behind his sister, he was hit by sweet, sickly smoke. The air was thick in the crowded main hall, where one of the acts was already playing. There was no stage and the large band were set up in a corner. His sister owned Black Uhuru and Third World albums, although she'd threatened him with a beating if he so much as touched them.

The only lighting came from the centre's strip lights which brightly lit the audience as well as the performers and left Marcus feeling exposed. The four of them weren't the only white people in the room, but they were in a tiny minority. Andrew and Mel left Marcus and Colin standing by the dance floor as they went to buy soft drinks from a trestle table bar. The centre didn't seem to have a licence to sell alcohol. Marcus bobbed awkwardly at the edge of the dance floor. Colin stood next to him, immobile, chewing slowly on the strings of his anorak. Reggae music was entirely outside his frame of reference.

Two young girls with neatly braided hair sipped Fanta from straws as they watched Marcus's attempts to dance and giggled, whispering to each other without once taking the straws out of their mouths. He blushed with embarrassment and was about to leave the dance floor when he felt someone place their hands on his arms. He twisted around to see Andrew standing behind him.

'Relax,' he said, which only served to make Marcus feel more uptight. 'We're here to have fun.'

Marcus could feel the warmth of Andrew's hands through the cotton of his T-shirt. Andrew gently pushed and pulled him to the beat. Humiliated and turned on in equal measure, Marcus had little choice but to try to move with him. Andrew danced easily, smiling, unaware or uncaring what people thought of him. His attitude gave Marcus confidence. The music was hypnotic. The thick smoke in the air made his throat dry and his head light. Marcus closed his eyes and imagined what it would be like to dance with Andrew every week. When he opened his eyes, Andrew was snogging his sister.

Vijay Khurana has been a presenter on Australian national radio station Triple J and a journalist for Germany's international broadcaster, Deutsche Welle. His children's chapter book, *Regal Beagle*, was published in 2014.

This story forms part of Vijay's collection *The Designated Optimist*, and was longlisted for the 2018/19 Galley Beggar Press short story prize.

www.vijaykhurana.com

Zenith
An extract from a short story

Tangerines and cheddar, not the most exciting car food. My wife Marie is quartermaster on this voyage across the island. If one of us asks she will unfoil, she will cut a polygonal piece of cheese, hand over a tangerine. Mine she peels: I am helming.

Count your segments, Marie calls to the back seat, twelve is lucky! Her mood expands to fill the space, we are on vacation, we are going to find the place of her great-great-grandfather's birth.

We being the rhizome of the family tree she has brought with her. It is secured with a hair elastic, safe in a cardboard tube in our shared suitcase. Behind us, all that we love: Console, who is smarter than he lets on, and our sparky little Journalist, who likes to prod life's hull in search of cracks.

That's superstition, Mom, Journalist says. She is not quite eleven. She has picked the word up, it is a jigsaw piece, she wants to know where it will fit.

In a way, says Marie, but that doesn't mean it isn't true.

Super-duper-stition, Console says, and we laugh. Super-duper-mega-stition!

He is nearly nine. The car has filled with the smell of tangerines.

A moment ago there were drystone walls on either side of this road – now they are replaced by hedgerows. An open field. Graves. A church. I see one half of the church door darkly open, nobody around. Briefly, I am able to watch us from the outside: I can walk from the churchyard into the road, into the wake of our rented Volvo. A dark grey fluid drips from the tailpipe, serrating the tarmac, as though the road were zippable, or unzippable. As the engine noise fades, the hedges and trees come alive again. Flitting blackbirds, their beaks orange against their black bodies. The rustle and still of last year's leaves. Earthworms, humus, cream-coloured bones. What to do now the car and the family are gone – go back inside the church? Burrow underground?

The vision scatters and I am easing my wife and children around a corner, covering the brake as my sight line decreases, doing all the right things. The transmission growls into second and Console asks Marie for a piece of cheese. He is polite. Our kids are polite. I can sense him wiping his hands on his trousers. I imagine the game's smeared screen, its lurid, habit-forming colours. He is wearing the headphones that came with my iPhone. They are his now, more or less. Journalist counts her segments, counts twelve. She doesn't trust herself (or perhaps just enjoys the attention) so she counts again. I tell her: Now see if something lucky happens to you.

We pass a playground, steel slide glinting, sand pitted with last night's rain, swing hand-roped from horizontal bough. The site must have been chosen for that perfect branch because there isn't much else around, no houses, just a field behind with some horses, a line of trees beyond that, signifying a little river or perhaps a lane.

Can we stop, Dad? We cannot stop. My daughter sighs like a tiny engine. The other one barely looks up from his screen. We have a swing at home, he says, a little wisely. And she: Not like that one, ours is plastic, and ours isn't hanging from a tree, it's hanging from a *metal frame*. Suddenly I want to stop and go back, or at least pull over and build a statue of her. Instead I say that we need to get to our destination, need to see the village her great-great-great-grandfather grew up in.

Why was he so great, Console asks.

Great sometimes just means big. And big sometimes just means old.

Marie feeds me, a few segments at a time, the sharpness pulling at my cheeks. White noise as I lower my window and spit out the pips, hiss back to gentle hum, no, it's not littering, they're just seeds. If you come back when you're eighteen a tree will have grown.

Will the swing still be there, my daughter asks spitefully.

You won't want to go on a swing when you're eighteen, says her mother.

We also have a bag of walnuts from a shop called Dunnes, which Console loved because we are also the Dunnes. But our nutcracker, brought across the Atlantic by Marie, who adores nuts, is, we suspect, still on the patio table at the School House Bed & Breakfast. With the kids asleep we sat outside in the evening air, cracking shells and feeling the rain's approach, wondering if there were any other guests and if we were disturbing them. My voice vibrated in my throat as I tried to keep it just above a whisper, a pleasing sensation. We didn't say anything much, just about the night and whether we would meet anyone who bore her family's name, the one she gave up in favour of my monosyllable (the family joke is that it's the sound to use when imitating the dramatic music from a horror film). She was O'Halloran, Marie O'Halloran, a perfect undulation until she married me. We must have left the nutcracker there on that plastic table, next to the upturned flowerpot we eventually realised was an ashtray. When I went to the bathroom I crept through our room, heard my children's duelling breaths. I didn't flush the toilet in case it woke them. We flushed it once, just before we went to bed, our mingled waste chemical-bright in there. The patio door slid softly shut and locked, the nutcracker still outside.

Marie has inserted three segments into my mouth, done slowly this time, with my two hands on the wheel, my mouth open around her fingers. Her pinkie touched my bottom lip. She has painted her nails – when did she paint her nails? I crush the fruit, it is four o'clock, the car's sun visor is down. Somewhere I have a pair of sunglasses, probably in my bag in the trunk. Marie says she saw a sign that read nine miles. Nine miles to her people's village. She puts her hand on my leg.

Where are we staying again, I ask, wanting to know if this is one of the nights for which we have booked an extra room. Usually we crowd in together, a double, a single (Journalist), a fold-up (Console, who is barely two years younger and complains bitterly). But we have added little breaks along the way, like the ones we take while driving. They come twice on this twelve-day trip. Marie scratches at my jeans and says through a half-yawn: It's the one that used to be a windmill. Her eyes are on the road. There is a teasing pause, then she says, You kids'll have your own room tonight.

Gross, says Journalist, who might be referring to having to be alone with her brother. But she has long been onto us. Marie has been quite frank with her, I have heard it. My turn to have this conversation has not yet come.

The Volvo arrives in a village of whitewashed houses, slate roofs. The church tower bodes somehow well for our mission, it has a parapet. Like a castle, Console says. Not for the first time, his New England accent (much stronger than mine) reminds me of the voices we've heard in this country. Marie is turned away from me, taking in the graves. Slabs, most of them. The odd Celtic cross. I put my foot down, lightly, then a lemon and green post office, a pub with flowers in great buckets outside. Continuing as though to leave the village, as instructed by our confirmation email, we find the windmill.

Brian, the owner, is ready to welcome us as soon as we step onto his gravel. He beams cream-coloured teeth, jovial, but keeps his hands in the pockets of his corduroys, and when I extend mine and say, Doug Dunne, it seems more than he bargained for.

The windmill still has its sails, though they are reduced to wooden frames that no longer turn. Brian shows us the chains that lock them in place, so they don't keep everyone awake with their creaking. The top level is the dining room. It has a circular balcony with wrought-iron tables and chairs, where breakfast will be served if the weather holds. Our rooms are tiny, partitioned spaces in the lower level where grain was once pulverised. Brian and his Slovenian wife Ana (Marie asks for the spelling when she hears it pronounced) live in the house behind.

They bought the windmill twelve years ago, when they moved from Dublin. They met in Ljubljana as students, but came together by complete chance a decade later, after the wall came down. It sounds like a story Brian has told many times. Marie responds not with the story of how she met me, but with a précis of our mission. Tomorrow we will look around the village, go to the church, look at headstones. She slips in her maiden name, to see if it will trigger anything. But Brian is not from here, and his smile hints at all the other Americans who have come here and done the same thing. Is there anyone we should speak to, an expert on local history? The priest might know something, there would be marriage records somewhere. Ana says: But isn't Father Michael on holiday? Right enough, Brian says, he's in Corfu. I didn't know priests went on holiday, I say.

Brian and Ana make dinner for us, lasagne, garlic bread, salad, fish fingers, peas. We play cards. I read my son a story at bedtime, pretending they won't each reach for their devices once the light is off. All of this is a prelude to being alone with Marie. She has been teasing me all day in tiny ways, making sure the thought doesn't leave my head for too long, making sure the driving doesn't tire me. We unpack as much as we need to, and with the bag of walnuts on the bedside table, the family tree leaning against the wall near the en suite, she unbelts me as we kiss. In her mouth I am full, relaxed, the mouth that ate lasagne at dinner, that steered Console away from a tantrum over a denial of sticky toffee pudding, the mouth that will keep saying her rounded maiden name to strangers in this place. O'Halloran. She is warm and she knows me. I look down at the hand around my penis, the burgundy nails, the wedding band, the engagement ring she picked out herself. Come back, I say. Come here.

We are a condom couple, we always have been. What's changed is that they have somehow ceased to be my responsibility. Marie packs them now in her washbag, along with tampons, toothbrush, make-up, razors, vitamins. She folds around my body the way we have practised, puts her teeth on my collarbone, holds me there like an animal play-fighting. She used to be loud when we lived alone. Since having kids, we've become librarians. Even if there were no one for miles, we would still be subdued.

We breathe into each other's faces. We love each other. My semen ends up knotted in latex, wrapped in a tissue, placed in the little bin beside the toilet.

The morning is no less bright than the previous day, though it is windy, and the decision has been made to serve breakfast inside. Silverware glints on tables edging the centrepiece, the axle running through the building like a skewer. There are other guests: a young couple who whisper close across their table, and what look like father-and-son hikers, booted and taciturn. Marie is strangely quiet too, letting me take charge of breakfast, issue mild threats to Console about there being nothing else until lunchtime and a big walk around the village before then.

Jasmin Kirkbride is a sci-fi and fantasy writer, with short fiction published in various magazines. Her work is represented by Sandra Sawicka at Marjacq and she is starting a PhD Creative and Critical Writing at UEA in autumn 2019.

This extract is from chapter three of *The Border Wife*, the first book in a dystopian trilogy told from multiple viewpoints.

jasminkirkbride@gmail.com

The Border Wife
An extract from a novel

JONATHAN

*The three most important qualities in a Youth Troop associate are
intelligence, ambition and loyalty. The intelligent will protect our families.
The ambitious will build our future. The loyal will be rewarded.*

—

Extract from *The Ray Protection Alliance Youth
Troop Handbook, Vol. 1*

'Good, but this time with more feeling.' Mr Grant sits back in his armchair
and closes his eyes, tapping his foot on the bare floorboards of the music
room like a metronome.

Jonathan starts again. He resists gritting his teeth, knowing the tension
would affect his grip on the bow, but *The Quarryman's Song* is a simple
enough tune and he can't figure out what he's doing wrong. Mrs Banyard
had always been happy with how he played it, though Jonathan is fast
learning that his old cello teacher's standards are not the same as the
RPA's. Of course he's grateful to her for helping him get the Youth Troop
Music Scholarship, but under the eagle eyes of Mr Grant, Jonathan is going
to have to up his game.

'The trick is to become one with the bow,' Mr Grant instructs. It's the
fifth time today this enigmatic phrase has come up, and Jonathan tries
once again to relax into his instrument, while at the same time retaining
proper posture. He runs through the lyrics in his head, pushing them
into each note: *Though breath deserts and flesh recoil, our bones will be your
final foil; for in that night beyond the sun, we shall renumber one by one...* It's
a nonsense song, just an old folk tune the quarrymen sing to keep their
pickaxes moving in time. How can he add feeling to that!

As Jonathan draws his bow across the last vibrato note, Mr Grant shakes
his head. 'That's enough for this week, Drucker. Really, you must try to
inject more emotion into your work. True musicians don't rely on technical

ability alone.'

'Mrs Banyard used to say all I had to do was try to create something beautiful.'

'Quite. Beauty comes from within, Drucker. Connection. Understanding. Not just comprehension, hmm?'

'Yes, Mr Grant.' Jonathan will figure it out during the week; for now the lesson is over, and he has to hurry to his Youth Troop meeting. Being in the Youth Troop was the whole point of getting the scholarship in the first place.

As he leaves Mr Grant's classroom, he checks both ways before starting down the long Music House hallway to the loos. He sneaks along the corridor, looking over his shoulder for the Short brothers, and using the displays on the walls to mark his progress. He manages to get past the general notices, the choral concert posters, and the antique electric guitar that hangs in a deep frame with a note about pre-Border instruments. Darting across the hall, he slips into the musty loos, locks the door behind him, and sighs with relief.

He dumps his cello and changes out of his school clothes. He began the process of applying to the RPA Youth Troop the moment he turned sixteen last year, desperate to shirk the nerdy label that had been bestowed on him by the Short brothers and cemented when he accidentally called Miss Dentman 'Mama' one fateful day in Upper Third. He still cringes when he thinks about it; that, and all the other myriad humiliations heaped upon him since. His preparation paid off, and he is now one of the youngest Youth Troop Associates. As he pulls on his uniform, its power seeps into him, and he forgets he's a nerd hiding from the Short brothers: he is a soldier in the war against the radiation that lies beyond the Border.

As a final touch, he takes his Youth Troop pin from his blazer collar and attaches it to the chest pocket of his uniform, then examines himself in the mirror. The uniform's pressed wool trousers make him seem taller and, if he squints through his glasses, the padded jacket makes his back look almost broad. The Drucker men have always been skinny and short, but with this uniform, Jonathan hopes he might be able to transcend his father's woeful inheritance. His body is already changing. They work out a lot at Youth Troop, and over the summer Jonathan's gained enough weight that he's finally been allowed onto the school rugby team.

He notices a rogue, wispy hair poking out of his chin and plucks it with his fingernails. He's going to have to learn to shave. Not that his appearance really matters: Mayor Goodwin is ugly as sin, and he runs the whole town. Jonathan's clever – cleverer than the other boys his age, or he wouldn't have been accepted into the Youth Troop – so he understands that your reputation is your power, not your face. That's why he's so diligent about his grades, rarely swears, and is always careful to ask the right number of questions. Never too few, never too many, and always appropriate. Considered. Not rebellious like his wayward twin sister. It's crucial to have a good reputation because that's how you become a fully-fledged member of the Ray Protection Alliance.

True power – not the kind that enables a bully to enforce a wedgy on a weedling, but the kind that will let you run life on your own terms – is gifted by the RPA. No scientist, politician or journalist is assigned without the RPA's approval, so if you have an Alliance Card, you have a ticket to the interesting and lucrative jobs, most glamorous dinner parties and, importantly, the pick of the ladies. His father's obsession with the printing trade can go hang: Jonathan is determined to reach the highest Alliance ranks, and the future is his for the taking.

Turning away from the mirror, Jonathan shines his boots. They are his pride and joy, and he has inserted thumbtacks into their soles, so that they click efficiently when he walks, just like Troop Leader Hewitt's.

Boots gleaming, Jonathan folds his school clothes into his bag, hoists his cello onto his back and grabs his schoolbag. He pushes his glasses firmly up his nose, nods to his reflection, and hurries out of the Music House. Here, on the outskirts of the town centre, he's still close enough to the Main Square to hear the gong in the Cathedral tower beating out five o'clock. He scurries down the street, sweat building between his uniform and his cello case. But he's getting stronger; its weight isn't as much of a bother as it was the first time he made this journey a few weeks ago.

Horse-drawn carts clatter past, their solar-powered headlamps like sunbeams in the gloomy autumn day. In some of the larger shops, electric lights pop into life, while candles burn in the parlours and kitchens of cosy terraced homes. Jonathan only has to get as far as the Townhouse & Sons bakery at the end of Gravel Street where Rob and Derrick will be waiting for him. Then he can relax.

'Hey, look who we've found!' Jonathan's stomach drops as Hank Short shouts at him. 'It's Dopey Drucker!'

Hank and Stanley Short saunter over to Jonathan from across the street and tower over him, reeking of tobacco smoke and snorting with laughter. He's rooted to the spot, like a rabbit in torchlight. Yet, once they get close enough to register his uniform, the Short brothers hesitate, hovering a few feet away. They're still giggling, but their eyes flick repeatedly to Jonathan's

RPA badge, and he knows they're too frightened to do anything.

'It's Jonathan,' he says.

'*Jon-a-than,*' says Stanley Short, not quite dropping his mocking tone.

'That'll do,' Jonathan concedes, screwing up his courage.

And he does something he has never done before in his life: he walks away from the Short brothers. He doesn't hobble crippled by a wedgy, or scuttle off covered in orange juice. He doesn't even curl into a ball and wait until they're gone. He just turns around and walks away – though the hand clinging to his cello case strap brushes over his Youth Troop badge, just for luck.

He takes one stride past them, then two. He can't believe he's actually going to get away with it, but with each step his breath eases: they're not following him. Before he knows it, he's waving to Derrick and Rob outside the bakery. Both boys are from similar moulds to Jonathan, from less well-to-do backgrounds than their fellow Associates, but all the more loyal to the RPA for that, coasting on their ambition and a modicum of academic success.

'Hey!' Rob says, flicking his floppy hair out of his elfin-featured face. 'Saw you run into the Short brothers back there – did you hear they got busted for selling tobacco on the big pitch earlier?'

'No,' says Jonathan, slightly disappointed that their restraint may not have been just because of his uniform.

'Yeah, but nothing's going to happen. They cause trouble all the time and nobody ever does anything about it,' Derrick says. He's the opposite of Rob, shorter even than Jonathan and round as a wagon wheel. His father wants him to take over the family bakery, but Derrick is the other music scholar from their year, and Jonathan knows he secretly wants to be a trombonist in one of the jazz bands that play in the upmarket clubs in town.

'You just wait, when we're in charge, idiots like the Short brothers won't get any free passes,' Jonathan replies.

'From your mouth to the RPA's ears!' Rob laughs. 'Come on, we don't want to be late and have to stand at the back like slackers, do we.'

The Youth Troop is divided into five parts, one for each of Finborough county's boroughs. Jonathan, Derrick and Rob all belong to the Northborough Troop, so their local Youth Troop Hall is in the north of town, near the fancy houses. Derrick always says it's so the private RPA School kids don't have to suffer commoners, though Jonathan's pretty sure that's the chip on his shoulder talking. As they make their way through town, they bump into other Northborough Associates from other schools, some of whom have come far enough to be riding their bicycles. Jonathan is awkward with his giant cello looming from his back, but Rob is so cheerful he draws people towards them anyway. Soon enough, Jonathan finds himself at the centre of a rowdy crowd of teenagers, all united by their polished Youth Troop badges.

Once they are all ensconced in the Hall, Troop Leader Hewitt emerges onto the stage, and they fall into a reverent hush. Jonathan salutes so hard his hand quivers.

'Good evening, Associates.' Troop Leader Hewitt's rough baritone booms out, the sacred Northborough Troop flag wafting on the wall behind him.

'Good evening, sir!' the Associates respond in unison. Usually at this point, the boys and girls separate out, the girls huddling together for their Junior Women's Alliance meeting. Jonathan isn't totally sure what they learn about in their meetings. Rumour has it that it's more than baking and cleaning. The women are the ones who understand the problems with Finborough's finite gene pool, who keep track of which citizens can and cannot marry, and calculate where and when dispensations for more than the obligatory two children might be made. Rob reckons it's all nonsense and they just talk about periods, but Jonathan – despite being unsure what periods are – doesn't believe him. The girls must do *something* in their meetings. Sometimes, he's amazed Rob passed the Youth Troop tests at all.

Today, however, Hewitt says they're going to do things a bit differently. 'Gents, you have to do your exercises as usual, giving time for our lovely Junior Alliance ladies to lay out beverages and biscuits for our break. Then we are going to come together to hold a session on identifying the Forsaken...'

Maya Lubinsky is the 2018 recipient of the Annabel Abbs Scholarship at UEA.

A long-time member of Punchdrunk Theatre Company, Maya has stowed her acting career in the freezer.

In *Y/N*, she explores the mother-daughter relationship, and the feedback loop between an individual and the world, which corrupts any sense of reality in the absence of cohesion.

mayalubinsky@gmail.com

Y/N
An extract from a novel

In a secure facility, a woman is under investigation. It has been many months since her family – her husband and their two grown daughters – turned her in to the authorities, their accusation being that she is not human.

In this chapter, the protagonist's friend, Cara, comes for a visit. Cara is the survivor of a severe traumatic head injury. Neural implants that bypass the damaged parts of Cara's brain save her from total and permanent disability.

A VISIT

'Your smile stands straight, good,' Cara said, hesitating in the corner of the mirrored room. 'But which is real life?'

Me and my reflections went up to Cara and steered her to the real chair. Her hand was chilly and soft as I pulled her towards her seat. Her scent was the smell of care and pride and flowers. I knew that it had come in a bottle, but it was hers nonetheless.

Cara's momentary smile flickered in all the mirrors.

'Darling,' Cara said. 'It's so nice to see you.' Her hand wafted across her face, like she was shooing a fly in slow motion.

'Thank you for coming,' I said.

In her sky-blue coat, her hair shoulder-length in strawberry blonde waves, her lips carefully drawn in red, she stood out like a Technicolor hologram in the monochromatic room.

'You look wonderful as always,' I told her.

'I have a lot of time on my hands, as always.'

'Regardless.'

'Have there been any developments here? Have they made a decision? Do you know when you will be out?'

'I don't know anything yet,' I said.

'Have you been OK in here?'

'I suppose it's all become normal. I sit alone in my cell, and then they fetch me to do a test. I do all sorts of tests. I don't know what I'm being tested for half the time. And then they feed me, and then I sleep. The temperature is well-regulated, that's one thing I'm grateful for – never having to be hot or cold. And the food is OK. And they even changed the soap in the dispenser because I was getting a rash.'

Cara remained motionless. She kept observing me, nodding slightly, as though I were still talking and she were still listening. She repeated her fly-shooing gesture again and again, and the minutes passed. I considered leaving her to recover herself in her own time, but I was mortified by her vacant eyes.

'Cara?'

'Hi, darling,' she said, a big smile resurrecting her features.

'Cara, are you OK?'

'Yes.' She nodded vigorously.

'Has anything happened? You seem a little... distracted.'

'Do I?'

'Just a little.'

'Well...'

'Tell me.'

'Well, I met a man on the train on the way over here.'

'You met a man?'

'Yes, just now.' She rubbed her forehead, the gesture blooming in the mirrors all around us. 'He asked me, "Are you married?"'

'That's rather forward,' I said.

'He asked about offspring. He said, "Eyes so blue." I was holding the pie that I baked for you. The man said that in his language there is a saying, "She is beautiful, and she bakes." He asked where I was going with the cake. I explained that it is a pie. He said, "I am a pie man, certainly. Sponge is for children."'

'You make a great pie.'

'The man's legs were splayed out, and his shoes stuck out into the carriage. He'd been reading a newspaper. Not the free sort of newspaper. But one of those newspapers you pay for.'

'The free newspapers are very sensationalist.'

'Yes. His paper was folded on his knees. When he sprawled his legs, it fell between them. It took me a while to realise that it wasn't me touching myself. When I looked down I saw that it was his hand on my thigh.'

'Oh.'

'It's confusing. I can't distinguish whether it is me or others sometimes.

I said to him, "I don't understand why your hand is on me. I didn't give you permission." He answered that I didn't protest, and I said, "I'm protesting now."'

'Good for you, Cara.'

The man asked why I was wearing sunglasses inside. He asked if I was wearing them so I could stare at people. He asked if I'd been watching him. He said he knew I could see him reflected in the train window.'

'He sounds horrible, this man.'

'Then another man stepped in. He asked me if I knew the horrible man. I said, "No," so he suggested that the horrible man leave me alone. The horrible man asked if I can't speak for myself, so I explained that I can't. I said I can't speak, that I don't know, that I can't know or speak. I explained that I don't have the full picture. That is, I have too much information. I can't distinguish between the noise of the train on the tracks and the words you are saying. I don't know what you are saying, not in real time, not fast enough to answer.'

'And what did he say?'

'"This is my stop anyway. Here is my card." And then – and this is the worst part – then my fingers gripped the card despite myself. I was only able to refuse the card once he was gone. I dropped it at my feet, by the forgotten newspaper. I had to look to make sure it was no longer in my hand. I feel terrible.'

'Oh, Cara.'

'Yes.'

'I appreciate you coming here. I know it can be difficult outside.'

'I am better at home. I am in control there. I can even play music. I can even listen to music. Next time I'll come by cab. The traffic is bad, that's the only problem.'

'Yes.'

'But even at home. I read a book and my thumb is on the page. Eventually I have to move it because I've reached the line that the thumb obscures. I have to move the thumb but nothing happens. I pause, waiting for the thumb to move. The thumb is obscuring my view and I cannot proceed. It is worrying, waiting for one's thumb to move. It is an uncanny experience. A splitting of the self. Waiting for a part of you that is not keeping up. But that is how I live now. I don't have a unified experience. Before, my senses worked in unison, and there was a coherent reality. It was highly curated but coherent. Now it's a big mess.'

'It sounds very difficult.'

'But as always, there is a silver lining.'

'There is?'

'There always is.'

'What is it?'

'It is that I can provide myself with sensations that feel like affection. If I want to feel less alone, all I have to do is this.'

Her hand adopted the role of a lover, stroking her face and resting on her neck. It smoothed back her hair and passed the thumb across her red mouth. The hand somehow even looked like a distinct entity, and I believed that it belonged to a stranger. As she proceeded, I tried to remind myself that Cara and the hand were one and the same, but I couldn't put them together again.

'Can you see?' she asked. 'It's like being touched by someone else.'

'Your hands are strangers.'

'Yes. It helps me when I am alone. This morning I was at home. Before that – last night – I went to buy groceries. Before that, I was at home. It was a nice afternoon.'

'Was it nice?'

'Yes. I heard the leaves in the tree. Cars drove by... I wanted to see a friend. There was laughter outside. Children too. The windows were all open.'

'Was it not too cold outside?'

'No, it was an unseasonably mild evening. Everyone's windows were open, not just mine. I cleaned the kitchen. I made tea. I looked out the window. I watered my plants. I drank water. The smell of roasting chicken came in through the windows. I cut some wood to size.'

'Oh, did you?'

'There is a minor step in the house. It prevents me from rolling my cart of tea and sandwiches. It is only fifteen millimetres, but the cart gets stuck. I bought a fifteen-millimetre threshold ramp and cut it down to size. I glued it to the floor using silicone. I watered my plants using a mist spray. If you wet the leaves, you avoid getting pests. I reached out to someone. This was on a dating website. I wrote a message. I tried to be interesting. I buffed down my nails.'

'That sounds like a nice evening.'

'I don't know, perhaps I spend too much time at home. In daylight, in the window across the courtyard from mine, I can see a reflection of my window. I can see in the reflection that my window is open, and beyond that reflected open window is a dark room. It is in that dark room that I sit. That space is visible to me – only barely. Beyond it is Cara. I want to go over there to see what things are like over there. To check whether it really is so difficult to sit there calmly.'

'Cara, the holidays are a difficult time for many.'

'Yes. It is a time when many people feel isolated.'

'It is a time when people are prone to overeating as well.'

'I used to struggle with my weight, before.'

'What about Rick? Have you seen him lately?' I asked.

'Yes.'

'Did you meet up?'

'Coincidentally, at the supermarket. He was there.'

'Was it nice to see him?'

'Yes.'

'That's good,' I said.

'He apologised for not being in touch. He said that after my accident he was afraid of my expectations.'

'Do you have expectations?'

'I don't think so.'

'Then it's all OK.'

'Yes.'

'He misunderstood.'

'Yes. He said the pressure was too great, so he wasn't able to want to see me.'

'That's a shame. He had it wrong.'

'When you get out, we can go somewhere nice. Maybe out to the countryside. Maybe abroad. To a resort. Somewhere warm.'

'That's something to look forward to.'

'You always have to have something to look forward to.'

The door slid aside once again, opening a single unreflective sliver in the wall. The guard stepped in, informing us that our time was up.

'This flew past,' Cara said. 'An hour is nothing. It is barely anything at all.'

SYLVIA MADRIGAL

Sylvia Madrigal was born on the Texas-Mexican border and graduated from Yale University in 1979. She is a candidate for the MFA in Prose Fiction at the University of East Anglia. *Unrequited* is the first in a series about the lives of great lesbians lost to history.

sylmadrigal@me.com

Unrequited
An extract from a novel

New York City, 1968
I loved her. More than I had ever loved anyone. The way I had seen heroin addicts love heroin: without regard for certain death.

When I met her at Salka's in 1931, I had known the beds of many exceptional women. My penchant for actresses was not a secret.

The path that led me to her, on that sunny June day on Mabery Road in Santa Monica, began at age seven, when I thought I was a boy. On the day I discovered I was not, I contracted a spiritual illness which would haunt me my entire life.

My mother, descendant of the Spanish Dukes of Alba, would have none of it. No daughter of hers could succumb to such a grotesque American malady. Her solution was simple: send me to a nunnery where I would be taught both the ways of womanhood and the Lord. My father's objections went unheeded and I was enrolled in the convent school run by the Sisters of Charity.

No sooner had I arrived than Sister Isabel enlisted me as a courier. I was to deliver written messages between her and Sister Clara. Not to be seen by the Mother Superior was my sole instruction. I spent my days looking around corners to escape detection, devising pretexts to visit each sister, basking in my secret status.

My joy was cut short when Sister Isabel called me into her classroom. She was staring out the window, frozen like a statue. I shook when I saw her contorted face. Mother Superior had transferred Sister Clara to China. For life.

I can still hear Sister Isabel's shriek when she bid farewell to Sister Clara. Falling to the ground in a lump, the sounds she made were the cries of death. When my moaning sickness returned, more virulent than before, my mother had no recourse but to withdraw me from the school.

On that glorious Los Angeles afternoon full of reckless sunshine, in the instant my soul laid eyes on Greta Garbo, I had no idea that Sister Isabel's cries of loss would one day be my own.

The truth is, I had seen Greta long before that day in Santa Monica. The first time was in 1922. Abram and I were in Constantinople and the Sultan had invited us for a feast in his palace.

When we got back to the hotel, I told Abram I needed to take a walk. I rejected his offer to join me. Before leaving, I made sure the box of letters from Eva was well hidden in the armoire.

Constantinople's skyline was gleaming like the Sultan's gold. The streets were bright with the colours and costumes of a thousand cultures. I could feel the heartbeat of the city, its citizens in motion, the gait of the elderly, the march of the young.

Eva was repulsed at the thought of me sharing a bed with Abram. I had no way of consoling her. The marriage was for everyone's sake. The world would not allow a woman like me to roam about the halls of society without the appropriate escort. Abram was my ticket to propriety.

Constantinople was overflowing with Russian refugees. They were huddled in makeshift shelters, starving, diseased, or dying. I heard a call to prayer from the minaret. I followed the emanation up the hill, for it seemed to be saying, *We, we know how to speak to the deity.* I had always been desperate to know God. I lit the specially blended cigarette with the gold coat of arms that the Sultan had given me for taking his photograph. I sat there inhaling the air mixed with tobacco, trying to make sense of my life as a woman who behaved in bed as a man.

I felt a small knot in my chest, the one born on the day Sister Isabel said goodbye to Sister Clara forever. There was a tightness, a softness and a twinge in it. Often I thought it might expand and explode. At other times it wound itself even tighter, like my mother's embroidery threads. I never knew what might activate it.

That day on the mount, it spoke of emptiness. How could I feel empty when I had secured the love of an internationally praised actress? Eva's play had taken New York by storm – she was the talk of both continents. We had even exchanged rings and sworn our allegiance.

And yet there it was, the knot in my heart. I had always trusted my body to deliver the truth. I thought my doubts would be quelled by reading the letters Eva had carefully marked for each day of my journey. What caused the irritation: the flourishing ascenders and descenders, the hearts in the margin, the tired phraseology of seduction? Actresses should not be allowed to write.

As I was sitting on the hill, smoking the Sultan's cigarettes, hearing the eerie beat of a thousand years of reverence rising from the minaret, I contemplated the tiny knot of pressure in my chest.

I was fifteen the first time I fell in love with a girl. Her nickname was Catiche. One day I found a note that she had left in my prayer book. Quiverings filled the area that many years before had proven to the doctor I was a girl. A poem erupted. That was the first time I took to the pen in response to a female combustion. I have since learned that unsated desires can be relied upon to detonate into verse.

I lit another of the Sultan's cigarettes and began my descent into the central plaza.

The knot in my chest lingered. I wanted someone who saw the world as I did, understood the layers of a life, the roaring madness, someone who saw how precarious it all was. Someone as wretched as me.

When I entered the lobby of the Pera Palace Hotel, I saw an apparition. She glided through the lobby like a Russian princess.

Who was she, and what was her native tongue? Before I could act, the vision disappeared. I accosted the first porter I could find.

'Who was that woman?'

The porter looked up from his duties toward the spot where the goddess had stood.

'I don't know her name, madam. They say she's an actress.'

The next day, as the train pulled out of the station, I was overcome by a rush of certainty. I would see her again. On a different shore.

New York City, 1900

I was seven years old and I was wearing my favorite sailor suit. My nanny and I were strolling down Fifth Avenue on a summer day.

As we neared our home on 47th Street, I saw a group of boys playing stickball. I pleaded with Katie to let me join them. Katie went up the walk and into the house. She turned to give me one last glance.

I ran up to the boys, excited to see them. I expected them to let me in the game as they always did. Without warning, Gerald was upon me. He looked angry. I could not for the life of me think why. Before I could ask him, he had pulled down his pants and was showing me the area between his legs.

'Have you got this?'

I pulled back in horror. I had heard of circus people who had physical deformities, but this was hideous.

'You're deformed!' I cried, terrified and worried for Gerald.

But Gerald was no longer the boy I knew. He seemed to grow taller as he yelled at me, making sure all his friends could hear.

'If you are a boy and you haven't got this, then *you* are the one who is deformed!'

All the other boys circled around me, and one by one, they each showed me the exact same deformity. 'Prove that you're a boy!' they all screamed. 'Prove it, prove it!'

I started to feel queasy. I knew I could not do as they asked. As their taunts grew louder, I felt sicker and sicker to my stomach. I broke through the circle and stumbled toward the front of my home.

Katie opened the door and I flung myself into her apron. 'What's wrong, my sweet?'

By now I was shouting wildly and crying. Katie tried to calm me as she pushed me toward my room.

'Where's my *mamá*?' I screamed into my pillow. 'I want my *mamá*!'

What felt like hours passed while I punched and screamed and tired myself out, only to awaken and begin the tantrum anew. Nothing Katie offered, milk, biscuit, apple or book, would help to pacify my outburst.

The door opened with a long, slow creak. Mamá was in her dinner dress, cooling herself with her finest lace fan. She took one look at me and motioned for Katie to leave.

'*Amor.*'

'*¡Mamá, mamá!* The boys! They say that I am a girl!'

Mamá knew this day would come. At first she had gone along with my desire to wear boys' clothes and engage in boys' sports. She thought it was a game that I would outgrow.

She spoke to me in soothing Spanish rhythms. She watched as I fell in and out of sleep, moaning like someone in deep physical pain. I imagine she thought I was undergoing some kind of delirium. She had no alternative but to call an American doctor.

He arrived within the hour. The doctor was slim and tidy, in a grey suit that made him look ill. He took a thermometer out of his weathered bag, shook it vigorously, and put it in my mouth. My temperature was well within normal range. He held my wrist and counted out the beats of my pulse. Again, nothing alarming. He coaxed me to sit up and talk to him.

'Did something happen to you, Mercedes?'

'Yes! The boys have told me I am missing something between my legs!'

'You are perfectly normal, Mercedes, I can assure you.'

'Well, are they the monsters or am I?'

Doctor Grant was confused. He looked at Mamá in puzzlement. This seemed a malady he did not recognize. With a nod, she encouraged him to continue the discussion. She had fared no better with me and did not want him to surrender so easily.

'Mercedes, you are a girl, and you have exactly what a girl should have.'

A long, unbroken yelp came out of me.

'Mercedes, it is much better to be a girl, I assure you. There are many advantages...'

The yelp turned into a howl. The doctor realized that he had no curative for this mysterious ailment. He was surprised to see me shoot straight up in the bed.

'Can you give me what they have, sir? Is there some medicine that can make this part grow on me?'

Doctor Grant's training must have included what to divulge to a patient. I could see him thinking, 'This is a child, for Christ's sake!' Nobody had ever told him what to say to a girl undergoing this particular strain of mental suffering.

'No, my darling. There is no such medicine.'

I deflated slightly, but then another wind of confidence blew through my tiny body.

'Could you operate on me?'

By now, the doctor must have felt the hopelessness of telling someone that a relative has died.

'No, dearest Mercedes. That is not a possibility.'

I shrank to my former size and withered underneath the blanket. Mamá let Doctor Grant out. As they whispered in the corridor, I began to hatch my next plan.

It was simple. I would ask God. I would steal away to church every day and pray to the Almighty that I might become a boy. I would do this with so much dedication that he would not be able to refuse me. Katie could help. Katie was very close to God. She talked to him all the time.

With this idea churning in my head, I fell into a drugged sleep. I had no doubt that one day I would awaken and peer under the blanket to see exactly what was true and right.

Ceci Mazzarella works in film/TV development. When she's not reading, editing or analysing other people's work, she's busy writing her own. Her first love is fiction and she's written several novels, most of which sit on the literary side of genre fiction, combining unease and humour.

cecimazz@hotmail.co.uk

Her Unquiet Sight
An extract from a novel

All the doors in every house they'd ever lived in weren't enough for Maat as she slammed through the new place, finally shutting herself in the bathroom. It was the only room with a lock. Her mother tried to follow, whining about money and spiritual responsibility and once-in-a-lifetime opportunities.

'Darling, please,' her mother begged, knocking on the door.

Maat shoved the laundry basket under the door handle, and grabbed a bunch of towels to cushion the bathtub as she climbed inside. A perpetual draught slipped under the window above the bath. She put in her headphones and tried to watch something on her phone, but it flashed red; she'd left the charger in her bag downstairs. Even half an hour with nothing to watch was better than having to talk to her mother about whatever had happened back there. She didn't believe in ghosts or crystals or Ouija or voodoo or angels or any other nonsense her mother felt like bringing into their lives, but not believing was a lot easier when she wasn't in the room with it. It was just her imagination, she reminded herself, overreacting in a creepy house with an old lady. It was her mother's influence getting to her. It hadn't been real. It couldn't be.

She had wanted to leave the minute they arrived and had thought being polite would make the time go faster. Getting the job would put her mother in a good mood and maybe blow over the incident at school. But that old woman had to offer money, her mother's weakness. There was no way Maat was going back to that house. Not for a million pounds, let alone five thousand.

Her phone died. She lay in the empty tub, headphones still in, and pretended to be somewhere else. She thought of all the bathtubs she'd been in, going back through the houses, ticking them off, testing her knowledge of the postcodes. They got hazy after the last five. Some of them hadn't had baths at all, just showers. The worst one had a bathroom they shared with two other families, both of whom seemed oblivious to their own filth; she couldn't stand waking up to someone else's hair in the plughole. She was glad to have left that place quickly, like she would be glad to leave this one. One day she'd set up on her own in a real house, one she owned, and she'd live there with a dog and a cat and she'd shoot down any medium who came knocking on her door. And she wouldn't give her mother the address. She would disappear so they could live their separate lives. She thought they would both be happier that way. Her mother never really wanted a kid, much less one with some guy she barely knew who had upped sticks at the first opportunity. But Gloria believed in the mystic powers of the universe – whatever they were – and if the universe wanted her to have a baby, then she had to have one. Fate, she called it. Maat wasn't keen on fate. It sounded like another excuse to play the victim.

'Darling?'

She hadn't realised her mother was still outside. She took out the headphones and listened to the rustle of skirts on the other side of the door.

'It's a lot of money,' Gloria said. 'But we don't have to do it. We really don't.'

She waited, sensing a trap.

'Just come out and have dinner with me. I'm going to make fajitas.'

'Do you have the ingredients?'

Her mother's voice brightened at the response. 'No, not technically, but you can have whatever you want, darling. You've been through so much today. I really do appreciate it.'

She sighed and climbed out of the tub. She moved the laundry basket and opened the door. Her mother fell inwards, chiffon tangled in a loose floorboard nail.

'Can we get pizza?'

Gloria stood and yanked her skirt free, leaving a clump of purple stuck to the floor and a webbed hole in the fabric above her knee. 'Whatever you want. I'm sure they do a salad or something for me.'

'Can you not just eat pizza?'

'I doubt there's anywhere around here that does gluten and dairy free. But you can clog your precious arteries with that stuff, if that's what you want.'

She ignored the impending hug and brushed past her mother, but Gloria caught her in the middle of the corridor, arms wrapped tight.

Maat waited out the hug and muttered, 'You know you're the reason I eat my feelings.'

'I know, I know. Blame me.' Her mother squeezed tighter. 'I love you, fatty.'

'Thanks for the eating disorder.'

She wriggled free and hid in her room while her mother went out for the food. She had unpacked her bedroom and half the kitchen by the time Gloria returned, hours later, with a tote bag looped on her arm.

'What's that?'

Her mother tipped the bag onto the kitchen table. One oven-cook pizza and some green salad. 'Pre-heat the oven, would you?'

Eyeing the box, she didn't move. 'I thought we were getting takeaway.'

Her mother laughed as she draped her damp coat over a chair. 'Not when you've just cost me five grand. Pizza's pizza, isn't it?'

'It's not the same.'

'No, it's not,' her mother snapped. 'It's a fraction of the price.'

She turned away, unwilling to have this conversation again. 'I'm just saying.'

'Well, don't.' Gloria made a show of setting the oven, scarves trailing close to the gas flame as she stuck her head inside to check it was lit. 'I've paid for your uniform, your school books, the deposit on this place and the extra charges from those con artists at the removal company.'

'All right, I get it.'

'Do you?' Her mother slammed the oven door. 'That one job would have covered over four months' rent. If you're going to cost me work, then I'll have less complaining out of you.'

'So much for "you don't have to do it..."'

'I didn't say you have to do it.'

'It bloody sounds like it.'

'I can't do this right now.' Gloria nursed her temple. 'I'm getting a migraine. I need to lie down.'

'Oh, here we go.' She said it under her breath, but she knew she'd been heard and there was no going back. She ripped open the pizza box. 'Something else to stop you getting a real job.'

Gloria shaded her eyes and drew a shuddering breath. 'I have a condition. It's very hard for me.'

She heard her mother's voice catch, but she focused on putting the cardboard pizza in the oven and didn't reply.

'It's really hard for me,' her mother said again. 'You saw what happened in that house.'

'That wasn't anything.' She stood on tiptoes, searching the cupboard for some condiments to disguise the taste of dinner.

'It was real!'

The force of her mother's voice made her knock a box of cornflakes out of the cupboard. They spilt across the floor and crunched underfoot.

'This, this is real.' Gloria's shirt was pulled away from her shoulder. 'You felt it too, I know you did.'

'I didn't see anything.' She longed to believe herself.

'We have a chance to help that poor woman and you don't even care. Who knew I'd raised such a selfish child?' Her mother's favourite guilt tactic.

'You don't want to help her. You just want the money.'

'I have a noble duty to perform.'

'So, you'd do it for free?'

Her mother snorted and readjusted her clothes to hide the ugly bruising. She busied herself with a salad dressing. 'We have to eat, don't we? You complain enough about that as it is.'

'No.' She had her mother this time. The chance to seize her own once-in-a-lifetime opportunity was too perfect. 'If your job's so important, if it's a "noble duty", do this one for free.'

Her mother laughed. 'You don't understand how this works. If I did one job for free, everyone would expect the same. Then how would we keep a roof over our heads, Miss Morals?'

'OK, then.' She cast around the room, finally finding the magnetic whiteboard and pen. She started scribbling. 'You take the job, I'll go with you, and I get to decide what we do with the money. All of it.'

Her mother hesitated, half a lemon raised in her fist, dripping over her iridescent painted nails. 'What? That's absurd. What would you spend it on?'

'I've got some ideas.' A proper takeaway, those gold trainers, a new laptop, and she'd still leave some for the rent, whatever her mother might have thought. The rest was for Canada. She knew the money wouldn't cover the school fees, but she needed a tutor to be in with a chance at the full scholarship, not to mention the application fees and somehow getting to London for the entrance exams. Then she could finally get away from this place for good, maybe even see Robbie again. Some peace of mind, that's what she would buy. A future her mother couldn't imagine. 'Maybe I'll give it all to charity.'

Her mother scoffed.

'It'll be proof.' She continued writing. 'Proof that this is a real, noble profession. You can even add Mrs Zee to your testimonies. I'm sure she's got some creeps in her coven looking for a cheap medium.'

'I'm not cheap and she's not a witch,' her mother said. 'Don't be so racist.'

'Witches aren't a—'

But that was one argument too many for one evening. Instead, she held out the whiteboard and presented her handiwork. A contract, albeit a rough one.

Her mother scanned the words. 'I don't need to prove anything to you.'

'Fine.' She shrugged. 'Then we won't do the job.'

'Now, hang on—'

'Sign it.' Maat slammed it on the kitchen table between them. 'Prove the money doesn't matter and I'll go with you. I'll do as you say. I'll wave burning sage and sacrifice a goat to Hecate, if that's what you want.'

'Well, what good would that do? Where would we even find a goat?' Her mother paused for a moment. 'I'd need to train you.'

'Fine.'

'You'd really listen to everything and not question my methods? I can't do this if you're going to be making inappropriate sacrificial references.'

'Yes, fine.' She took the board back and made a squiggle, her signature. 'See?'

Her mother snatched another pen from the side, and scrawled a combination of her initials and a rune at the bottom of the whiteboard. 'Agreed,' she declared. 'We'll be a team on this one. It's not going to be easy, but we'll do it together. When it's all over, we'll wipe the slate clean just like this board.' Her mother followed her gaze to the smudge at the bottom of the whiteboard. 'What?'

'That's a permanent marker.'

Shandana Minhas is the author of the novels *Tunnel Vision*, *Survival Tips for Lunatics*, *Daddy's Boy*, and the novella *Rafina*.

shandanistan@gmail.com

In-Laws from Space
A short story

It's a hot day in Karachi. The loadshedding is unrelenting, and the generators are running out of petrol. Everybody has the windows to their inner demons rolled down. I am at the salon getting my nails done when talk turns to in-laws. Put any number of Pakistani women around a body of water – river, sea, sink, pedicure tub – and talk always turns to in-laws.

Reema says hers are awful. Kiran says hers are wonderful. Palvasha says hers are all right.

I say mine are from Space.

Reema says hers are so awful, if Hum TV based a drama on them everyone would watch it. Kiran says hers are so wonderful, if Hum TV based a drama on them nobody would watch it. Palvasha says she can't see what all the fuss is about. Women who obsess about their in-laws are bored women with nothing better to do and life would be better without their dramatics.

Reema changes her mind.

I say mine are from Space.

Palvasha thanks me for a timely illustration of the precise point she was making. She tells the other women I'm probably turning a perfectly nice mother-in-law into an outlandish character just to get attention. I say my mother-in-law is a perfectly nice character; she's just from Space. Palvasha says I'm doing it again.

Even if her in-laws were horrible, Reema chimes in, she wouldn't run them down the way I'm running mine down. Kiran points out that woman-on-woman negativity keeps all women down. The girl doing my manicure tugs my cuticles hard enough to make them bleed; she wonders out loud whether I would be a happier person if I tried a different nail colour.

I break the rules of salon friendship and invite everyone home for tea.

Confusion and panic ensue. A pedicure girl overturns the tub while her client – a person of smallish size – is still in it. Kiran tips Reema 500 rupees. The salon owner offers everyone a free face polish. Palvasha stares at me. I stare back. To blink first would be as humiliating as crying during an underlegs wax. I tell Palvasha it's OK, I understand that people are afraid of meeting my in-laws, them being from Space.

Let's go! she snaps.

They follow me to my car. On Sundays there is no traffic, and the driver is parked in the shade of some *Concarpus erectus*. Their desiccated seed pods float gently down to the ground. I miss the *Mangifera*, I say, and the *Syzigium cumini*, even the *Cocos nucifera,* but nobody responds. It is as if they don't care that the species is invasive, that a monoculture is extending roots across their cities. Palvasha and Reema walk in the centre of the road, like they have never walked down one before. A zephyr teases their hand-painted silk dupattas behind them in passing; they look like vultures, hoping to savour the carcass of my social life.

I sit next to the driver. Kiran, Reema and Palvasha start getting into the back. There is tumult: the pedicure girl has come along! Reema tells the girl she has left a bag inside and will the *jaani* go get it; Go! the women yell as soon as the door slams.

On the way, Palvasha asks if I'm a local. I say I have always lived in Karachi, but my in-laws are from elsewhere, of course. She asks if they have all converted too, or just my husband. I reply it hasn't been an issue because their physiology allows for the effective inhalation of both nitrogen and oxygen.

The others perk up before our gate. I don't like to brag but we have a nice gate. It is about twenty feet high and there is razor wire on top of it, which runs along the boundary walls for a quarter of a mile in either direction. This pleasing symmetry is broken at artful intervals by sentry towers, buttressed by organic sand in recyclable khaki bags of hemp fibre; at the top of each tower are very fit men in navy blue uniforms, drawn from indigenous ethnicities: Sindhi, Baloch, Punjabi, Pathan, Seraiki, Mohajir, Kashmiri, Hazara, Kalaash, Sheedi... we have them all. The colour of their uniforms complements the green and white of the concrete blocks placed at regular intervals along the base of the perimeter. People are always vaulting the blocks, jumping the acid moat, ringing the bell and asking if it is the Saudi Embassy. And the gate guard has to say, No, if it was they would be dead already.

Our house is a normal-sized house. It has three storeys, six bedrooms, seven bathrooms, two kitchens, and a basement home cinema. The servant quarters are on the roof and there are expansive lawns all around, with a kitchen garden by the wet pantry and an ornamental vegetable garden alongside the guardhouse, which has an artillery gun on the top. Both house and guard house are sandstone glaze, to reflect ecologically sensitive architectural practices.

Our foyer is dark. After you, Palvasha says into the gloom.

OK madam, the houseboy replies.

Our morning room looks onto topiary. Three *duranta erecta* children with wings sprouting from their shoulder blades and tiny horns rising from their craniums pad across the lawn, one with a baby on her hip. A heptapod rises above a mongoose in *ilex dipyrena*. A dolphin in *arborvitae* springs out of a pond after a flamingo; one slender leg is trapped in the mammal's mouth. In the centre of the display, offering a parcel, stands a Tellytubby postman in *buxus sempervirens* with a circle of snarling Asian wolves around him. Early in the morning, with the sun rising behind them, the figures glow. By nine, if you squint, they are on fire. And at noon, as now, with the sun directly overhead catching the red of the *rhododendron arboretum* snaking down the postman, dotting his neck, his leg, it is like looking out onto some bleached other world. My husband says it reminds him of home.

I ring the bell for the maid after asking the houseboy to tell the cook: tea for six. She is the 76th we have hired. Her prior job was wet nurse for quintuplets, so she has experience of body servanting. Her uniform is a tinfoil helmet, army boots, a tool belt with sacks of five kinds of roses and a portable chainsaw. I whisper, Let my mother-in-law know we have guests for tea. She puts the tinfoil helmet on, and scatters petals before leaving the room.

Palvasha asks if I am convent-educated.

I say the flowers would then have been plastic.

When my mother-in-law comes in, the odour of ammonia wafts before her. The women's nostrils widen a second before their eyes. Salam Ami, I say.

Salam *beta*, are these your friends? What beautiful friends. She speaks through the maid's mouth, and settles into a chair. Her legs cross demurely. One hand rests on the other in her lap. Two tentacles tuck into her armpits. A third lies on the wrist of the maid, who is standing behind her; skin to skin contact allows Ami to manipulate human larynges. A net tulip shalwar exposes a carefully polished expanse of her iridescent scaling. The faces of her male offspring are screen-printed onto her silk kameez, a rabid psychedelia of anemones. Red lipstick outlines her beak. There are kohl pencil ticks over all three eyes. She has made a real effort; I hope my non-friends will try to like her.

They cannot stop looking at her. Her presence weaves through the room like a needle, sewing all lips shut. Silence falls so often in our home I am frequently tempted to stop picking it up, but now is probably not the time.

I ask loudly if anybody wants cake. Nobody responds.

I do! Ami reaches a tentacle across the room, picks up a piece of cake, whisks it to her open beak and drops it in. Her mottled throat begins to bulge, the colours of her tentacles change rapidly, an ammonia-scented wind flips our hair and then – PLOP!

A perfectly formed turd lies on the petals.

Kiran starts rummaging in her bag. We have to leave, she says, I have just remembered there is an emergency parent teaching meeting to discuss the Comparative Hate Literature curriculum today.

And my teenager, Reema adds, has a dentist's appointment to remove his baby teeth.

Palvasha smiles angelically.

I'm afraid I can't let you, I say, now that you know my mother-in-law defecates diamonds. I wait a beat, before pressing the turd with a cake fork so a koh-i-noor winks at us. I remember to smile so they know I am joking.

Is that...? Kiran asks. Could it be...? Reema muses. But how...? Palvasha frowns.

Cultural differences, I explain.

They nod. It's not a judgemental nod reserved for things that aren't local culture, like sales tax, jeans, or women laughing, but an understanding nod, for things that should be: potable water, medical care, free diamonds. They have time for another cup of tea after all. They admire the striking patterns on my mother-in-law's kameez. They all laugh when Ami tells a knock knock joke.

Knock knock.

Who's there?

Are these your eyeballs? Ami picks up cake pieces. I'm going to eat your eyeballs. Ami eats the cake pieces. Plop! Plop! Diamond turds fall on the carpet. Laughter falls like the blood of the topiary postman.

At lunchtime I nudge the women towards the door. My husband always comes home to eat; it isn't safe for them to stay. I stand by the entrance steps and wave them through the gate. They smile and wave back. Already, the glamour is rewiring their memory, rolling the tentacles into braids, the third eye into a classical-style pendant, the scaling an unfortunate reaction to locally sourced shellfish. They will remember only what is necessary. And now they know how much my mother-in-law's excrement is worth, everyone they know will know too. I will be featured in social pages, invited to coffee mornings, yoga weekends, milads, charity balls and themed dinners. There will be multiple robbery attempts at our house. Next time I go to the salon, the girls will fight viciously for the finish line of my brow.

They will, of course, all wonder how a shy, plain nobody like me ended up with in-laws from Space. I will let them wonder. My phylum of the species does not have adequate sociologically deterrent features. I would not wish to draw humanity's attention to it.

CARMEN MORAWSKI

Carmen Morawski is a Santander Scholarship recipient at UEA. Her poetry translations have been published in the *Hayden Ferry Review* and *Lunch Ticket*, and her prose has been recognised by the *Words and Women* competition and *Bellingham Review*. She is writing her first novel, *In Solidarity,* a coming-of-age narrative set in Communist-era Poland.

carmen.morawski@gmail.com

In Solidarity
An extract from a novel

Please note: Tata, Babsia, and Dziadek are the Polish equivalents for Papa, Grandmother, and Grandfather, respectively.

CHAPTER SEVEN

June 1974 – A small town in Southern Poland

Anna brushed the dry leaves off the smooth granite and stood aside as her father poured water over the stone. He worked from side to side, tipping the bucket carefully to make sure the entire surface was covered. When he finished, Anna rubbed a cloth over the wet slab, working in small circles to loosen the embedded dirt and flattened leaves. She stepped aside once again, and her father poured a second coat of water over the tomb. Then, after rinsing the cloth, Anna wiped the stone clean.

She stood up. 'Better, Tata?'

'Much better.' He smiled and put his arm around her shoulders. 'Your mother would be pleased.'

Absent and perennially benevolent... Anna sighed and picked up one of the glass lanterns. 'Do you have the candles, Tata?'

Her father produced three candles from his satchel, and lit the first one for Anna to set into the lantern. She carefully placed it inside and then did the same with the other two. She lined all three along the head of the stone and stood back. 'June 20, 1959,' she read.

'Hard to believe it's been fifteen years.' Her father shook his head and made the sign of the cross before closing his eyes. Anna did the same, when a warm breeze rustled the leaves above her.

I'm sorry.

That voice. It had been a long time since she'd heard it. But maybe it had been her imagination. She waited to see if she heard it again. Nothing. Her imagination then. She crossed herself and tried to collect her thoughts, but no prayer would come. Her focus was elsewhere now. She waited, listening for the voice... but there was nothing. Just the rustling of leaves.

She strained her ears... and then, there it was.

I'm sorry.

Her mother's voice. She'd heard it clearly that time – as if she were standing beside her. Anna opened her eyes. She didn't believe in ghosts, not really, but there *were* things that sometimes happened, the kinds of things she couldn't explain. She wanted to believe she'd imagined the voice, but the words had been clear.

It fitted the stories Babsia sometimes told her, and not just the stories, things she'd witnessed. Like the evening Babsia was telling Anna about the moment her mother had died, and just as she was describing how peaceful her mother looked, how relaxed her face was... in that moment, the teacup Babsia was holding in her hand shattered. Just like that. Her mother's favourite teacup. Without warning. Even now Anna shuddered to think of it. But not Babsia. She crossed herself without a word and got up to mop the tea from the table before taking the fragments to the sink. The next day she glued the teacup back together and set the damaged heirloom on the dining room sideboard, centring it conspicuously below a large landscape her mother had painted.

As a child, Anna had usually heard her mother's voice while she was drawing, and almost always in the little hiding room, but it had been a long while since she'd heard it, and never in the cemetery. But today was special, the fifteenth anniversary. Still, they'd done what they always did on this date, visited each of the family gravesites, cleaning each one and leaving a single candle to burn. As always, they'd started with Uncle Stasiu's and Great Aunt Jósefa's on the far side of graveyard, then this year, Dziadek's, leaving Anna's mother's for last. In previous years, Babsia had been in charge, pulling the weeds surrounding each grave and doing most of the cleaning, but she hadn't been feeling herself since Dziadek's death.

'It's strange to be here without Babsia. And...' She didn't know if she could say it. 'And... Dziadek.' She took a deep breath. 'I miss him,' was all she could manage – even after a year – as if he were away on an extended journey.

'I do too, Myszko.'

'Babsia said we need to put everyone together someday... in a big crypt.'

'It takes money.' He shook his head. 'And she wants to be near Dziadek when her time comes.'

Anna didn't say anything. She didn't want to imagine the day she would have to care for Babsia's gravesite. Or her father's. She thought about the graves she'd seen in the small wood. A strange place. The large stones in disarray, many of them toppled over, with tall grass and weeds all around.

'It would be better if they were together, easier to take care of when it's just me.'

'That won't happen for a long time.' Her father hugged her close. 'A long time. Besides, you'll be married by then, with a family of your own.'

The mythical family of the future. She wished she could see it as clearly as her father. 'Tata...?'

'Yes, Myszko?'

'Is that why Mama is here?'

'What do you mean?'

'I found a place. A cemetery, I think. But it was a mess, the stones pushed around, and the writing... It was different. Not like anything I've seen, not Polish, not Cyrillic.'

'The old Jewish Cemetery,' he said quietly. He turned to look towards the entrance, and Anna saw that another couple was coming up the walk. 'What were you doing there?' he asked as he started to gather up their things.

Anna picked up the bucket and poured what remained of the water over the nearby wild flowers. 'I don't know...' She didn't want to explain, but if she hadn't been looking for it, she might never have seen the place. In front of her nose but hidden. 'I was curious, and, well... I'd heard there was an old cemetery... And... I thought I might find the names of my grandparents. But then I couldn't read anything.'

'It's in Hebrew.'

'The place is a mess, Tata... and no one is taking care of the graves.'

'There's no one left.'

'Is that why...'

'What?'

She hesitated. 'Why Mama isn't buried there?'

'No.' The word was heavy, impatient. 'She's here because she was a good Catholic.'

'But... wasn't she also Jewish?'

Her father shook his head. 'Anna, how many times do I have to tell you?' She could tell he was trying to control himself. 'The only people who thought she was Jewish were the Germans.'

'But what about her parents? The Babsia and Dziadek I never met?'

'Myszko! I've told you a million times, they—'

'Were taken away,' she finished. Anna looked across the cemetery as they walked towards the entrance. She'd scoured every inch of the place. Two summers ago. The summer Zbyszek had told her about her grandparents' house. Almost a year of sneaking around, so no one would notice what she was up to. But she hadn't found any Kwiatkowskis. Then she'd heard about the old cemetery in the woods.

'Taken away.' As if that were enough to explain. He was hiding something. She was sure of it, but she could never push him past those two words. But where had they been taken? And why hadn't they come back? It was as if she were supposed to know, and it wasn't OK to ask. All her life, so many secrets. Not just about the war, but about what had happened after. As if what you didn't know couldn't hurt you.

They had almost reached the cemetery entrance when Anna stopped in front of one of the big family crypts. 'Do you think this is what Babsia wants?'

'No,' her father said shaking his head. 'Not anything so big.'

'It *is* enormous,' she agreed. The walls of the monument were tall, almost a foot taller than she was, and dark with age. A large moss-covered crack threatened to bring the entire structure down and a healthy stand of fern had rooted itself into the sinking foundation. Chiselled above the door was the family name, 'Majewski,' and on each side, a tablet engraved with the names of the dead. Anna began to read them out loud, 'Elżbieta Majewska, Adam Majewski, Stanisław Majewski, Danuta, Miroslaw, Anna, Maria, Antoni...' She stepped back. 'There are so many of them, Tata. But I've never met any Majewskis.'

'An old family.' He looked away. 'Gone now.'

Anna nodded – best not to ask.

'Do you want to take a walk, Myszko?' He looked at his watch, then at the sky. 'It's not likely to rain, and I could use a walk in the woods.' He set the bucket he was carrying behind the open cemetery gate, 'We'll pick these up on the way back.'

Anna gave him a quick kiss before setting her cleaning things into the bucket, and the two of them started towards the forest. Though not quite noon, the sun was nearing its peak and the shadows it cast made the two of them look like dwarf versions of themselves. 'Look at how small we are,' said Anna, pointing. 'You have to get the shadows just right, Tata. Or your painting will look funny.'

'My daughter, a scientist *and* a painter.'

The pride in his voice was nice, even if it did embarrass her a little.

'This sun is wonderful, isn't it?' He stopped to pull off his sweater and wrapped it around his neck. Anna did the same, but wrapped hers around her waist to make the most of the sunshine. 'Tell me,' said her father, 'how do you feel about September?'

Anna looked across the fields. The rye was about knee high and the wheat not far behind, so that summer's green hues were just beginning to dominate the brown furrows of early spring. 'I'm going to miss all this...' She sighed. 'And of course, you and Babsia,' she added. 'But the art academy – it's in Krakow.'

Her father didn't respond immediately. 'I hope you get in, Myszko,' he said, and paused as if considering what to say next, 'And I believe you have a good chance, but French Philology – it wouldn't be so bad, would it?'

'Would you rather I do French, Tata?'

'I want you to do whatever makes you happiest. But...' He sighed. 'I think you may have more opportunities with French.'

They left it at that, neither of them speaking as they walked past several of their neighbours' fields, most planted in wheat or rye, and it wasn't long before they passed one of the Opoles' fields where Marek and his father were working, slowly making their way down a row of potatoes. Marek was ahead of his father, crouched low as he examined the leaves, stopping occasionally to stand and put something into the jar he'd tied to his waist. Potato beetles. Anna had collected them many times and in just the same way. Behind him, carrying a manual sprayer and misting the air above each plant, Pan Opole looked as if he were walking in a private cloud of early morning fog.

'That DDT can't be good for him,' said Anna's father.

'Marek says it kills the beetles.'

'That may be,' he said shaking his head, 'but it may kill his father too.'

'Is that why you don't spray our field?'

He nodded.

'Is it true the beetles are from Colorado, Tata?'

'I'm not a scientist... but that's what they tell us.'

'Do you think the Americans really brought them?'

'Hard to know. But does it matter? They're here now.' He nodded in Marek's direction. 'But more important than that, Anna... how are things between you and Marek?'

'Tata!' How he could shift a conversation. 'From beetles to Marek!' She focused her eyes on the path before her.

'He's a nice young man,' her father continued, 'but—'

'I *know*, Tata,' she interrupted, doing her best not to sound annoyed. 'He's not going to university.'

'But do you love him?'

It was a good question. One she wished she could answer.

Madeleine Morgan grew up in London. Before coming to UEA, she worked as a ballet dancer and has a degree in Philosophy from the Open University. She writes short fiction and is currently working on her first novel.

morganmadeleine@hotmail.com

Salt City
Extract from a short story

'When the waters had fallen, not all the way but most of the way, we came back with boats, three of us. We rowed through the streets of our childhood.'

The camera loved Pablo almost as much as he loved it. Gone was the watchful quality. By turns, he was charming, humble and full of pathos. He sat, one knee hooked over the other, in the blown-out window of the butcher's shop, pressed shirt and flat cap matched to the blue tile counter. A newspaper lay folded in his lap. Laure increased the depth of field to capture the salt and water damage. Nico crouched, just out of shot, holding the microphone.

'How did it feel to come back after all that time?' he asked.

Laure pulled the focus back to Pablo. Time was a strange word to use here. It had been suspended. Nothing moved except the wind which burned and exfoliated. When the town had risen from the bottom of the lake, it had aged far more than the twenty-four years it had been submerged. The ruins seemed ancient though the breeze block and twisted rebar located them firmly in the last century.

'There wasn't any one thing to feel,' Pablo said. 'We began at the church and worked outwards from there, finding our houses, the ice cream parlour, the bakery. The dance hall was gone. Much was gone. Not as much as now. Things are still falling. In the night, I often hear them. I don't know why you don't hear them in the day. Maybe I'm just busy with other things.'

Laure zoomed in on Pablo's paper. The date was that day's but she and Nico had passed no one on the road to come out here. Besides the three of them, the town was deserted.

'You must have felt like Noah in the Ark,' Nico said.

Pablo leaned back. Where his shoulder brushed the wall, concrete crumbled.

Nico glanced at the lintel over their heads. 'Can you tell us about the salt?'

Pablo shifted to look at the lake. More dust fell. 'The water, they analysed it and said it had curative powers. The first patients they brought here to be healed were horses from the racetrack. They were beautiful animals.'

'What about the salt extraction? When did that begin?'

'We became a famous spa town. Everyone started to come here. Important people. Famous people. I met them all. It was an honour for me. Even people from the radio came.'

During their research, they had watched nine, maybe ten, interviews with Pablo. Certain lines he reused and there were embellishments that had crept in over time. Nico had been against approaching him but few people they'd met had been willing to go on camera.

'Now the music, that I do remember,' Pablo said. 'There were special shows, at hotels, for the tourists. It wasn't meant for us but we'd listen from the street. I had a friend who worked as a waiter and sometimes he got me in. It was the first music I heard. Later, they brought other kinds of music and the people changed.'

This was also lifted verbatim from two other documentaries. Nico didn't interrupt but he had the next question ready. 'So, the flood in eighty-five, do you have any theories about what caused it?'

'I'll tell you about that when we get to the church.'

Nico pressed his thumb against the corner of his notebook. Months of research fanned under the pressure. Laure wondered if it had been wise to tell Pablo that he was the focus of their story when their real interest was the question Nico had just asked.

'Can you tell us about the meeting where the evacuation order was given?'

One of Pablo's dogs ambled into shot and yawned. It needed a dentist even more than he did. He scratched it behind the ears then pushed its nose away gently. 'The municipality called the meeting. The whole town packed into Plaza San Martin.'

Laure took the pen from behind her ear and wrote *P. San Martin* on the back of her hand. In Carhue, people had given the names of other squares; one said the town hall.

'The dam had already broken when they came to talk to us, only in two places, where the structure was weakest. The water was coming in, but slowly.'

She scribbled *date meeting*. This was another point of zero consensus.

'We thought they would fix it,' Pablo said as Nico eased the microphone towards him. 'We thought that the rest of the dam would hold and the lake would recede. Even I believed this.'

Many of the buildings were whole. Some missed a wall. In others dry grasses grew through the rubble of roofs caved but you could still see the neighbourhood it had been. Even with the bakery shelves warped and wild flowers springing from cracks in the fishmonger's counter, it was easy to match to photographs from the thirties. What Laure couldn't picture was Pablo, with a moustache, queuing for his bread or attending the meeting in the eighties.

Nico cleared his throat. 'Why didn't the municipality repair the dam?'

'They said it was impossible.'

'Did you believe them?'

'When the rest of the dam gave, the water came and covered everything. It rose a centimetre an hour. Sixteen days.'

'Do you ever wonder if they could have stopped it?'

'No.' Pablo was still talking directly to Nico. 'What's the point?'

It was the same answer they'd been given every time they turned the camera on. Even when the camera was off, people would imply but never state.

'Once the decision had been made, things moved quickly. The army came, firemen. Everything of value was taken to the train. I was one of the last to leave so I saw it all. They marked where they thought the water would reach and that's where it came up to.'

'*Who* predicted the level that the water would rise to?'

Pablo ran his thumb across his lips. 'The engineers.'

Laure wrote *engineers* on the inside of her wrist. It made sense that there had been engineers but this was the first mention of them they'd encountered.

'Can you show us the mark they made?'

Pablo straightened his shirt. 'I can show you many things.'

They switched to handheld camera. Nico carried the equipment while Laure filmed Pablo cycling through streets. The dogs followed, their movements almost choreographed as they fanned out across the road and fell back into his slipstream.

The first stop on Pablo's tour was the rusted carcass of a sports car, marooned in the mud. From there they went to a playground that groaned in the wind. The dogs took turns running up the seesaw, tipping its balance. Then it was the statue of a crescent moon that cradled the real sun; Pablo showed Nico the best angle. Next was a concrete staircase. Whatever it had led to was long gone but the steps featured in four other documentaries. Pablo climbed it slowly, dogs at his heels.

Nico rummaged in the bag for a bottle of water and went to talk to Laure while she filmed. 'You want to take a shot at him?' he asked, when he'd taken a deep swig.

'What kind?'

Nico's smile was tired.

She pressed pause and took the bottle. 'You all right?'

'Frustrated,' he said, 'sweaty.'

'You want to see some of what we've got?' she asked. 'It's good.'

'Show me the bit where he talks about the meeting.'

Laure scrolled through the clips. She felt Nico relax as they watched it together.

'I bet you a beer, there's no mark,' he said when the play icon reappeared.

'And I bet you a beer, there were engineers.'

The ruin Pablo took them to was marked by a single layer of white bricks – half architect's plan, half crime scene. 'This is where the engineers made their mark,' he said, pointing to where a wall once was.

Now there was nothing but blue sky and heat shimmer. Laure panned back down and walked slowly around the perimeter of the building.

When they got to the church, Pablo asked if they had a light meter but when he had it in his hands he wasn't sure what to do with it. He gave it back and spent some time arranging the mise en scène. After two aborted takes, Laure lied and said the memory card was almost full. Pablo went back to the cracked font and began over.

'These bricks were made by my father. There was an Italian architect, the cripple...' Pablo paused to gauge their reaction. 'It was his idea to build the church here. My father tried to warn him; he said, "Look at the earth. Where there is salt, there was water. Cycles repeat. Water will return to this land by the eighties." I was only five, but never forgot coming to the church that first time.'

Laure was more careful to control her expression. There had been no Cassandra-like father in Pablo's previous tellings just as there had been no millimetre-perfect engineers but as she began to edit the footage in her head, she thought back through the other documentaries they'd watched, the cuts that had been made. Pablo had told them, twice, that he'd never seen any of the films he starred in but she wondered now whether this was true.

'No one believed my father,' Pablo said. 'I was still making bricks, right up to eighty-three. They're piled up, waiting for someone to use them.'

'So this land had flooded before?' Nico asked.

Pablo whistled for the dogs. 'It was a long time ago, before I was born.'

'If your father knew about it, there must have been others – the town planners, the investors would have had access to that kind of information, no?'

'Knowing is not the same as believing.'

'But there would be records...'

'All records were lost in the flood.'

Before Nico could ask his next question there was a loud rustle; the sky filled with flamingos – hundreds of them, absurd and beautiful, legs dangling before they straightened out for flight. She and Nico stood, faces upturned as it rained pink feathers. The birds completed two large loops then landed on the far side of the lake.

'That's...' Laure stared at the empty sky, 'incredible.'

'They live here with me,' Pablo said. He whistled again for the dogs and called them by name. When they appeared they were both wet. They circled but didn't come close.

Nico waited. 'Could we talk now about whether or not you think environmental damage was responsible for the flood?'

'I'm no scientist,' Pablo said. Sensing that something was slipping away, he picked a brick up from the ground and began to talk to the camera, 'If a brick was made by my father I recognise it...' His thumbs moved, unconsciously, tracing and moulding the form. 'I know the markings, the work. I can say this was made by his hands.'

There were more bricks, more names. He led them to a place with no walls or shadows; sun flared off the whiteness; wind blasted through the audio. When he finished talking, Laure squatted down and stretched out her back muscles. She had salt in her hair, her ears, her mouth. Nico crouched behind her and began to work his thumbs along her spine.

'What do you want to do?' he asked quietly.

Pablo stood, observing her silence as she thought about the shower waiting for them at the hotel. 'I have photograph albums I can show you,' he said.

Nico's hands stopped moving. Laure steadied herself, small stones biting into her palm as she ducked to put Pablo between herself and the sun. Silhouetted, he looked tiny in the ruined nave with its roof of sky.

'You drink maté?' she asked.

'What kind of a question is that?'

Laure laughed. 'Nico's dad grows it. We brought some.'

Tess O'Hara, from Bath, writes romance, coming-of-age, and satire. She was runner-up for this year's Brighton Prize and won the University of Roehampton's Editor's Choice Award. Her stories and poems have been published in *Adjacent Pineapple* and three Fincham Press anthologies.

tess_ohara@hotmail.co.uk

Sleep Tight Vlad Skutnik
An extract from a novel

Cairo Jones is campaigning to be Putney's new Labour MP. She begins volunteering at a homeless shelter and is drawn to young, Romanian Vlad, but represses the attraction for five chapters...

CHAPTER SIX

Today I am not hosting a table. I am on sound. Music hasn't played in the homeless shelter since Christmas Day, so I've asked Alex if I can try to work the church's impressive sound system. I've connected my iPhone to a black cable. Now I stare at knobs on the sound mixer. I look underneath at wires, at plugs, and everything is switched on and I am frazzled.

The guests are coming in, passing by me to find tables, filling out the makeshift canteen. Vlad drops his sleeping bag and duffel on the other side of the sound desk. How embarrassing that I volunteered for a job I know nothing about. I fiddle with some dials. Vlad looks at me with a *what are you up to now?* face.

'Hey, you're a tech dude,' I say. 'Will you have a look?'

He steps around and into the sound nook with big, youthful steps. 'What are you trying to do?' He looks at my phone, the playlist *Cairo's Favourites*. A song is playing but only inside the phone's head, because I can't connect to the system. 'Ah, play music. Nice.'

He clocks the speakers around the room, eyes flashing like they have bluetooth, then bends down and looks under the desk. I step back to appreciate his arse. He stands, turns the volume dial that I put on high back down, then walks towards a closet door with wires coming from it. I follow him because I am on sound.

We enter a miniature room full of wires, switches and little lights, odd books and obscure sermon props: a bag of seeds, a plastic fish, and a basketball. Three oranges tied with red ribbon are loose on the floor. *Golden Guideline number four: don't go into any part of the building alone with a guest.*

Vlad runs his finger across the switches on the wall. I kick an orange, stand behind him, and the door shuts. He's so close that the button on my jacket is touching the wool of his jumper and I can smell black coffee on him. He turns one switch on, then off again. I have no reason to believe that he fancies me or feels our closeness as more than a slight awkwardness. He turns another switch and the second verse of *Hard Rain* by Lykke Li plays from the main hall. I put a hand on the door knob as he turns around.

'Well done,' I say. 'Thank you.'

'You're welcome.'

He glances at the door knob, my ready hand, at me. I look down and pass the orange to him. He kicks it back. We stare at our feet, cool, worn trainers and vegan-leather brogues, and his long-on-top hair dangles to tickle my forehead. Still looking down, I feel his eyes on my face, so I lift my chin. He's close. I lean in. He kisses me. He was going for a peck, but I rest my nose against his and lick his mouth open. His hands come around my waist and I cross mine behind his head. My body is so much smaller than his and his coffee tongue is bigger than mine, dark-roasted and strong. I try to be closer to him than I already am, my fingernails digging into his jumper, my tongue....

A metal clatter brings me back to the room. We've been here too long, considering the music came on a verse and a chorus ago. We should have delayed pressing the switch. We could have been struggling in here this whole time and for a few more minutes, just trying to find the button, techy guest helping a clueless volunteer get the sound going. I pull away, turn the door knob, breathe for a second, then open it.

'Thank you, Vlad,' I say loudly as we step out. 'I'll let you find a table.'

He wipes his mouth like he's been eating bolognese and leans into my ear. 'Where's *your* table?'

I force myself not to look around us for prying eyes.

'I'm doing washing-up now.'

'OK, see you,' he says. 'Thanks for all the help.'

In my first week here I would have loved to do the washing-up, so as to forsake food and chat to labour away for a good cause. Now I'm used to hosting. Even today, a part of me wants to sit, talk and pick at a meal, trying not to smile when I meet Vlad's eyes, but it's a gift that I'm on washing-up. It's best that I hide.

I watch him walk away, savouring his taste in my mouth. He chooses a table at the back of the room and sits. I step behind the sound desk and turn the bass down and try to turn myself off but even the concept of bass is hot. I check there's a decent range of songs on my playlist. Not too much The National or The Smiths. No excessive bad language because we're in a church. The Lykke Li song didn't sound too sexual when I added it to *Cairo's Favourites* and it probably didn't to the men and women eating in the well-lit main hall, but will have to Vlad, with my tongue in his mouth. I add some Avicii because that's the kind of stuff he likes. He nods his head along when The Last Shadow Puppets come on, meeting my eyes as I head for the kitchen. Be careful, Cairo. Tread slowly.

Stepping into the kitchen, I realise how tense my body is; I feel over-caffeinated. Toby is washing up too. He has a soapy bath ready for the first pots, though the kitchen team are just taking the soup vats into the main hall.

'Cairo!' he says. 'You're doing this with me?'

'Yes. Awesome,' I say.

As soon as the cooking team finishes with some chopping boards and knives, we get to work. The warm water calms me. The creamy fishy smell of the pie grounds me. Toby asks about the campaign and I dry my right hand to show him my new Facebook profile. He says the red jacket suits me, and he'll 'like' the page when he gets home. I ask about his lawyerly life and try to show as much interest as he shows in my work. But he sounds bored of his own voice until he mentions that he's working on a project on the side. Mary drops a saucepan the size of the sink in front of us.

'Oh yeah?' I say, grabbing the better sponge and claiming the saucepan as my job.

'It's a bit niche,' he says.

'Do tell.'

'Well, I'm launching a gay Christian dating app.'

My mouth drops open, but I snap it shut. I don't want him to assume wrongly that I'm shocked at the idea of gay Christian dating or to assume rightly that I thought he fancied me.

'That's – brilliant,' I say. 'That's a brilliant project.'

'Yeah,' he says. He looks around for something to wash up but finds nothing, then he reaches to the bottom of the sink and starts picking out bits of food. It's upsetting to see keen Toby so shy. 'I mean, I'm on Christian dating sites of course, and gay dating sites, but it's hard to find—'

'Both together.'

'Yeah, and there probably aren't that many of us. Out of the closet, I mean. But I figured, if we can get lots of us in one place, that's a start.'

'Definitely. And I'm sure everyone who does fit into that demographic will be really grateful that there's a platform.'

'That's what I'm hoping.'

I tip the saucepan, letting the dirty water spill into the sink, then upend it on the side. Toby grabs a tea towel. I feel embarrassed for misinterpreting his political fervour as a crush. At least I didn't tell anyone I thought he fancied me.

'Have you dated non-Christian guys?' I ask, then worry that's too personal. 'I mean, I'm agnostic, so I'm just curious.'

'I *have.* But it's not what I want long term. I don't want to compromise. I want a three-person marriage, me, the guy, and the Holy Spirit. Sorry, that's quite...'

'No. That makes sense. Good for you.'

The kitchen team rushes through steam, taking pies out of the oven and stirring last-minute spices into the vegetarian surprise to get that yellow colour popping. Toby and I have one dish to dry.

'I haven't really told many people about it. I mean, the app's in development, but, yeah, I haven't chatted to people here about it.'

'I think it's a great idea. You'll have to keep me updated.'

'Thank you. Thanks.' He takes the pan to the shelves and comes back. The second soup pan arrives, and he takes the lead. 'Anyway, are *you* dating anyone? No? Fancy someone?'

My heartbeat quickens. Did he see us going into the closet? Did he guess? No, he's only trying to direct the chat away from himself. He's scrubbing a mark on the pan over and over, making conversation.

'No,' I say. 'I'm boring. Actually, I went on a date the other day but it was with this intense man who only spoke in rhymes. Really, I'm focusing on the campaign. It's quite consuming.'

Toby's walls are coming down, but all I have for him right now is one persona, the young aspiring politician. I'll confide in him, sure, when I fancy someone who doesn't attend the shelter. You have to tell people outside of the circle, people who won't report you to the safeguarding officer.

'Sure. I can imagine,' he says. 'Do let me know if I can ever help with flyering or, I don't know, anything you need volunteers for.'

I'm relieved that the conversation is now in safer territory, but it's hard to talk about flyers when I can still taste Vlad on the tip of my tongue.

'You're just *such* a power volunteer,' I say, and he laughs. 'No, thank you so much. That's really kind. I'll let you know.'

When I leave the kitchen with pruney hands, the corridor is bustling like it's Easter Sunday. The women who stay at the shelter make their way upstairs to their bedroom. I spot Vlad queueing outside the loos, toothbrush in his pocket, rubbing his face with a wet wipe. The square covers his whole face and he presses his eyes.

'Boo,' I say.

He scrunches the wipe in his hand and smiles at me, sheeny. 'You have good taste in music,' he says. 'Everyone says this. I tell them, Cairo is the DJ. And I am her tech bitch.'

'Glad we've got our roles clear,' I say. 'I did add some electro on your behalf, though.'

'*You* have good taste in music,' the guy queueing in front of Vlad says to me. 'The electro ruined my night.'

We laugh.

'I will hold my music favourites to myself next time,' Vlad says.

'I'll see you later then,' I say to him. 'Sleep tight.'

'I will. Sleeping bag tight.'

I walk into the hall, letting his sad, witty comment settle in my memory. Solange's *Cranes in the Sky* plays. It's one of my favourites, like all of tonight's songs. I'd like to enjoy her chill melody on my way to the vestry, but men are starting to sleep, so I pull my phone from the cable. I return to the closet and flick the switch Vlad turned on, letting my finger linger on the ridge, then trip on an orange. My knee bangs against the shelves and I laugh as I lift myself up.

Tasha Ong grew up in Brunei, Singapore and England. After completing a BA in English Literature and Creative Writing at Brown University in the United States, she moved to Paris where she worked as a photographer, teacher and translator for eleven years.

tasha.ong@gmail.com

Until I Break
An extract from a novel

It was my idea to set the paper planes on fire. My idea, too, to bet on how many seconds they would burn – an addition to the game that made us lean farther out the window than ever before, forgetting our fear as we pointed at the ashes fluttering to the poolside, forty-five floors below. It was the summer holidays and every afternoon Simon came up to the penthouse from the apartment he lived in with his father on the ninth floor. He wasn't allowed to sleep over because I was a girl and because my parents were always away, but afternoons were all right because Effy would be there, cleaning or cooking upstairs in the kitchen as we played in my bedroom on the level below. I knew that Simon hated fire, and that he was terrified of heights, but I'd egg him on, making him hold the burning plane between his shaking fingers, making him blow at the flames.

'Scaredy cat,' I'd taunt him. 'Are you even a boy?'

At times, the planes plummeted. At others, they sailed towards distant apartment blocks. And every time, Simon and I sat a little bit closer, the timid heat of our bodies spreading through our sides. Over countless afternoons and years of sunsets, we continued throwing burning planes at the Singapore skyline, messages meant for unknown saviours. At ten years old, we were playing by the window. By the time I was fifteen, our games had moved to my bed. One year later, I walked back into the room to find his imprint in the bed cover, and though I didn't know it yet, he was gone; he had fallen from the window, while I was upstairs in the kitchen making tea.

At the inquiry, they asked me all kinds of questions. What time did Simon Starling come to the penthouse that day? Where were my parents when it happened? When, precisely, had I realised he was gone? They wanted place names, units of time, yes or no. They weren't interested in the questions that mattered. Shouldn't they have been a little curious about what Simon and I were talking about that afternoon? Didn't they want to know the reasons we'd been fighting before he died? But I couldn't have answered their questions, even if they had asked the right ones. I was in shock, they said, and they left me alone. Accident or suicide, the report stated, but a forgotten story kept whispering, hidden in the shadow of facts.

Simon Starling: one metre eighty-four centimetres, blond hair, blue eyes, Caucasian, seventeen years old, male. Body found at the poolside of apartment block A in One Arcadia Heights, Arcadia Road, Singapore. Time of death: between 4:22pm and 4:35pm, June 16th 1999. Cause of death: cranial blunt force trauma. Last person to have seen him alive: Alexis Langley – one metre seventy-five centimetres, brown hair, brown eyes, Eurasian, sixteen years old, female. Alexis Langley: liar, lover, cheater, sinner; guilty, repentant, praying to be saved.

It's my seventeenth birthday, the dead end of the summer holidays, and Bella has come over to the penthouse. I didn't want to celebrate, or to think about the days that have passed since it happened – forty-eight to be exact – but here we are, sitting side by side on the bed in the guest room, a paper shopping bag filled with gifts on my lap.

I look down at the presents, then sideways at Bella's face.

'Well, what are you waiting for?' She thrusts her hand into the bag and fishes out a long, rectangular object. It's wrapped in purple crêpe paper. Loose pieces of sticky tape catch on her fingers as she puts it on my lap. 'Here, start with this one.'

A knot hardens in my throat. I should be grateful that she's sitting here, beside me. I shouldn't be thinking about how Simon was going to take me to The Cranberries concert tonight.

I smile. 'You didn't have to get me anything.'

She rolls her eyes. 'Just open them, will you?'

I unwrap each gift slowly. A brand-new pair of Speedo goggles ('So your eyeballs don't fall out from all that swimming'). Pots of nail polish in *Milkshake Blue*, *Go Bananas Yellow* and *Paint the Town Red*. A shiny purple notebook. And finally, a mix of songs that she recorded to a minidisc, its small plastic case decorated with fragments of sunsets torn from magazines, their frayed white edges zigzagging a psychedelic sky. Circles cut from photos float across this background like balloons: Bella and I, tanned and pulling faces, squinting at the beach in Sentosa, at her house, at the penthouse. Most of them were taken in ninth and tenth grade, when Simon was away at boarding school.

'You didn't have to,' I say.

'Too late,' she says. Her smile fades when she sees my face. She wraps her arms around me, and holds me as I cry.

Upstairs, I mix her a vodka with soda water, then make myself a vodka and coke. I hardly eat these days so I figure the extra calories can't hurt.

We walk through the kitchen and on to the laundry terrace, then duck under a sheet billowing from a clothes line. There are two stools near the edge of the terrace. Beyond a low wall, the city glitters, a kaleidoscope of skyscrapers, dressed up and indifferent.

Bella takes out a packet of Virginia Slims, but I stop her from lighting up when I hear a noise. Effy back from running errands? I slip under the sheet and move towards the kitchen, but no one's there.

'All good,' I tell Bella as I settle down next to her again.

She takes a cigarette, then passes me the pack. 'What's the problem? I thought your mum knew you smoked?'

'Well, yeah,' I say. There's no point explaining why Effy's the one I'm hiding from. Because for everything that Bella and I have in common – one Asian and one English parent, a dad who left before we turned ten – there are differences too. For starters, Bella's never had a live-in maid like Effy. And her mum is always at home, breathing down her neck.

She lights up and takes a nervous glance behind me. 'Where is she anyway?'

'Carmen? She's in Phuket.'

She makes a face. 'It's so weird you call your mum by her first name.'

'That's how she wants it. *Mum* makes her feel old.'

We smoke without talking.

'Seventeen,' Bella muses. She cocks her head. 'What do you want to do tonight?'

What do I want? To slow time and swim through it backwards. To wake up and find Simon beside me, dense and warm between the sheets.

I shrug. 'Let's get shit-faced.'

She raises her glass. 'Only one more year until you're legal.'

Later, Alexis and Bella go out to a bar with some popular girls from school. One of the girls makes a comment about Simon that Alexis takes personally. Alexis goes off by herself, gets drunk and meets a boy on the dance floor.

We dance together for one song, then two, then he pulls me to him and we move in time to the music, his hands on my shoulders, his hips against my hips. The crowd swells, then his mouth is on mine, his tongue on my lips. We edge backwards and he pushes me against a wall, pressing against me. A wave of nausea. His hand slips over my ass. I push him away, but he catches my wrist.

His eyes are grey pools. 'Where are you going?'

I make a drinking gesture then walk back to the bar, stopped by that sick feeling in my stomach. I turn around, away from the dance floor, and down a corridor. Instead of the toilets, I find a small pool room where a game is in full swing – a Malay man with a shaved head against a wiry Chinese guy with tattoo-covered arms. Behind the pool table, some Chinese girls and a Malay biker wearing a death-metal T-shirt watch from a sofa.

Dad used to play pool. I didn't play much, but I would watch him. He said I had 'a good sense of strategy', those were his words. I stand in the doorway, fixing all my attention on the game until the nausea passes. Tattoo-arms seems to be winning but shaved-head doesn't look worried. When he finally gets the turn, he pockets ball after ball, then misses his last shot, almost as if he meant to. A fat Chinese man who's been watching from the corner walks to the sofa and whispers something in the Malay biker's ear. They shake hands and money passes between their palms.

At the table, tattoo-arms has taken back the turn. He looks down at his remaining two balls, no idea that he's being hustled. He has a green solid next to a corner pocket, a purple one next to a side pocket. Images flash through my mind. The bright green tables in the billiards room at the Tanglin club. Dad pointing at the different parts of the cue ball, explaining how to make it spin. My heart quickens.

I walk to the table. 'Aim here,' I say, pointing to the side of the purple solid. 'You can send it to the left – maybe get both balls in.'

He looks me up and down, as if I were naked. 'What's your name, girl?'

I step forward and try to take his cue, but he moves just before I can grab it.

'I'm serious,' I say. 'You're going to lose.'

I reach for his cue again, but he pulls back. He says something to the fat man in Chinese and the girls on the sofa laugh.

Blood rushes to my head. I turn to them. 'I'll give him three hundred bucks if I miss.'

More laughter. The fat man looks at me, thick lips thinning into a smile.

I reach into my handbag and shuffle around for some bills. 'See?' I take out some fifty-dollar notes, count them, then reach into my bag for another. 'Three hundred.'

For a moment, nobody moves, then the fat man murmurs something in Malay and tattoo-arms offers me the cue. I put the money back in my bag and bend over the table. But as much as I try to block out the sound of their laughter and the tinny beat of techno, I can't focus on the shot. The line of the cue lifts off the table, doubling before me like a harp string.

A cold hand on my arm. Someone pulls me backwards, away from the table. Jeering. Laughter.

Bella takes the cue from my hand and gives it back to tattoo-arms. She says something in Malay, her voice high. The fat man laughs. She walks towards the door, but I don't move. Behind me, tattoo-arms is taking the shot. He leans towards the table, right at the place where I was standing.

'What's wrong with you?' Bella hisses, beside me again. 'Let's go.'

As she pulls me from the room, I twist around. Tack tack. Tattoo-arms turns to look at me, his eyes like black stones. Both balls. I was right. He got them both in.

Troy Onyango is a Kenyan writer and lawyer. As a recipient of the Miles Morland Foundation Scholarship at the University of East Anglia, he is working on a novel and a collection of short stories. More information on his work can be found at troyonyango.com

troy@troyonyango.com

Beach Boy
A short story

Afterwards, we take a stroll on the beach while sipping our madafu and thinking of what to say to each other, but our words are the things we swallow and forget to spit. The sun is slinking down the horizon, half submerged in the ocean, and the water looks as if a fiery liquid has spilled on the surface, replacing the calming blue with a deep shade of orange. Seagulls fly in a circle then break away into a V-shape and back again into a circle. Their squawking sounds fill the air, and the wind blows eastwards, distorting their song. We walk on in silence, consumed by the sounds around us and the unsaid words trapped in our throats. The water slaps gently on the shore and our feet part the coarse sand rudely. He turns to me – his right eye slanting to look at me – and he asks, 'Do you still love me?'

I take a long sip from my straw and swallow hard, the sudden gulp of the liquid almost making me choke. I cough lightly and breathe in the salty air that smells of dead fish. I let out a loud sigh. My answer is formed in my head but not yet ready to leap out. I speak. The sound of the world drowns my response, and when I turn to face him, his figure is a silhouette floating, gliding down towards the bend where the palm trees sway and hug each other as if in fervent prayer. I want to shout and ask him, 'If I say yes, will I see you again?'

Something about the way he leaves tells me this is another story that has no ending.

I throw the green coconut shell to the ground and the ocean swallows it alongside the straw. Left to myself, I think about heading back to my hotel room, but the silence in my hotel room makes me think of death and sex as if the two are the same thing. And now that Theo is not coming back to me – I know, I know – there is no point rushing back. I know I am bound to find messages from him when I get back about how I always call him when I am at the coast just to *use* him for his body. I know he will curse me and call me selfish, but as always, I will remind him that I never force him to come to me. Furthermore, I will remind him that he is the one who keeps texting me asking when I am coming down to Mombasa to see him.

I play out the confrontation in my head and decide to take a walk along the beach, further down towards where the dhows can be seen waiting for the tourists who want to catch the late sunset.

The cool wind licks my scalp and the nape of my neck. I rub my hand on my shaved head to shield it, but the gentle assault continues. I walk on. A black polythene bag swims in the water, and a heron dives to catch it before realising its folly and trying to spit it back into the ocean. A herd of quacking birds circle the heron as it gets even more entangled with the polythene bag. The wind changes direction and blows southwards. I shield my face against it, my eyes still trained on the heron struggling to set itself free from its snare. I think it serves the bird right for trying to grab some fish from the shoal, but then I imagine that I was the heron and suddenly I am filled with pity and immense sadness and my chest tightens because of the bad feeling that's washing all over my body. I wish I could fly so I could help it, but instead I stand at the shore, the water teasing my feet, and I feel helpless.

From the corner of my eye – to my left side – I see the figure of a young man slightly taller than I am and with a chest the size of a boulder walking towards me. His hair is locked in thick tufts that have formed into dreadlocks not from styling but neglect. His faded denim trousers are rolled at his knees, and he walks with an exaggerated sense of swagger in the shallow part of the ocean where the froth rises, the water cleaning his feet and the sand making it dirty at the same time. He stops beside me and follows my gaze upwards where I have turned back to watch the heron falling lower and flapping its wings with less energy and determination than before. He points to the heron and asks me if that is what I am staring at. I nod, without looking at him, and he says in a sombre voice that the heron is going to die. What he actually says in his sing-song Swahili is that the heron is dead already. I remember my straw floating in the water, and my throat constricts, and my limbs feel weak with so much pain, for I too have contributed to this. I ask him how he knows for sure the heron will not survive. He tells me, 'The Ocean is dying and everything with it.'

I click my tongue, sigh and turn to face him even though my eyes are at the level of his chin. I notice the hair on his chest that looks like an aerial view of the Congo forest. He has a rugged, borderline-attractive look that I preferred early on when I was in my forties – before I met Theo. I try to make a conversation and ask him what he does, and he laughs in a way that sounds like a dry cough.

'You're not from around here, are you?' he asks.

'No, I'm visiting. I'm from Nairobi.'

'Ah, nilijua tu! We ni wale wa Bara.' He teases and switches his accent into something I have never heard before in my life, but I know it is how people from the coast imagine that the people from the capital like me speak.

I look at the sky just in time to see the heron drop down into the water like a comet. The sound is brief and distant but my body clenches when I hear it. The ripples on the surface of the water tell me this stranger's prediction has come to pass. The wind is still. There is so much silence around; it is as if the world has died alongside the heron.

'Watafuta nini huku?'

His voice reminds me that he is still here, still standing a few inches away from me with his skin that smells of the salt that remains when the water from the sweat has evaporated. The childlike squeak of his voice makes me think of the first time I bumped into Theo at a club in Lavington and spilled the drinks on his all-white linen attire, and he told me I was a clumsy piece of shit. I stared at him in silence as he hurled insults at me, then in a strange turn caught himself mid-sentence and apologised right afterwards. I offered to replace his drinks and take him shopping for a new set of clothes the following day. That was almost ten years ago and Theo was no longer the impatient young boy, but the one person who knew and understood how to love me. He would never hurt me, not intentionally, not even the day he announced that he was moving out of Nairobi.

'Huku hakukaliki,' he said – when he meant, *'This city does not sit well with my spirit.'*

I turn to the stranger next to me and tell him that I am looking for nothing at all. He shrugs and tells me, 'Sawa. But I know everyone who comes down here is looking for something.'

He looks like he has been around these shores longer than I give him credit for. I smile and ask him how old he is. He forks his fingers through his matted jet-black hair and he tells me, 'Is that what you need to know? You can ask for weed, cocaine, women to fuck until your dick hangs limp, anything really and you choose to ask for my age? Kaka, una mchezo sana!'

He laughs and this time it sounds different, like it is emanating from a different person, as if he has been replaced by a younger version of Theo. I want to scoop his laughter as soon as it leaves his mouth, cup it in my hands and keep it with me for a long time. He keeps laughing as if he knows his laughter is pleasant to hear. The water too is silent.

'I am not into women really,' I tell him, and I hang my head low as if weighed down by my confession. I do not wish to see how his face has changed so I choose to look away, into the water, which has turned black as if poisoned by death.

'Ha, ungesema hivyo – you should have said,' he says, 'I can get you a beach boy for a commission.'

I want to walk away before I make a mistake, but I stand and listen to his proposition.

'Unapenda the slim ones ama you like the ones with muscles?' he asks.

One could think he is describing an animal, something that merely exists for its flesh.

'Kama tu wewe,' I tease. Just like him.

'Ah kaka, una hela ngapi?'

I think of a random amount, something that I can give easily if at all he is serious with this.

'Twenty thousand,' I say. It is only after I have said it that I realise what a huge amount it is, but money has never meant much to me; I have always had it from my father who toiled all his life to make sure I had the best. Also, I spent all those years working in the ministry of finance so I could afford whatever I wanted. I have always thought that life is too short and you have to enjoy your hard-earned cash. Especially now that I feel old and things don't come to me so easily.

'Wallahi!' he exclaims as if to verify my offer and also to express disbelief.

'Yes.'

'Kaka, mimi nitakufira ukitaka. Maana mimi si shoga lakini hela ni hela.'

I am not gay but money is money – his words ring in my head. I watch him and wonder why I could not have just agreed to move to the coast with Theo. Why I insist on cradling loneliness in Nairobi when I have my Theo, always patient with me, always loving me. I listen to the lulling sound of the ocean. To the distant songs of the seagulls. To the silence of the heron inside the water.

I must tell Theo that, *The Ocean is dying and everything with it.*

I walk fast towards my hotel. The sound of the man's feet behind me is the only thing I can hear.

Hale Öztekin-Cuss, born in Turkey, holds a BA in Russian Literature and a PhD from UCL, where she teaches academic writing. She has also studied and worked in psychotherapy. Hale's connected short stories explore the psychological cracks in women/children when sandwiched between the Anatolian traditions and the new. Her story, *The Tea Party,* appeared in *Gains and Losses* in 2019.

hale.oztekin.cuss@gmail.com

The Death of Dodgeball
A short story

Esin's dodgeball team runs backwards. The opposition throws the ball, aiming at her. They want to land a hit, eliminating the best player. She moves sideways, ducks. Zeynep gets struck.

The rival team shouts, 'You're dead!'

Zeynep leaves the game. Now there are only a few girls left. Can they win? Esin seizes the ball, runs to the middle line and throws it as hard as she can, aiming for small and agile İnci, who dodges the ball. But when it hits the ground, she catches it and immediately starts to run. As İnci cocks her arm back, ready to throw, Esin knows that she is now the target.

'Oh no.' Esin's feet are flat on the ground.

Just as the ball arrives at her chest, the school bell rings.

'I'm saved,' she saunters towards the rush of students who are headed for the pupils' staircase. Only the teachers and parents can use the spiral one with the green banister.

From the corner of her eye she can see the almost-empty playground. Some girls are talking about moving to a co-ed school. What is it like to play dodgeball with boys? Difficult to imagine, but it may be good to be in the same school as her brother when he grows up.

It is the third period, and she is due in the language laboratory with the rest of sixth grade. She climbs the stairs beside Zeynep.

'I can't wait till the next break,' Esin says, and wipes the sweat off her forehead. She's good at dodging the ball. Being part of a team is fun.

'I'm dead you know.' Zeynep pulls up her knee-high socks.

'İnci never dies.' Esin laughs. 'I'm going to ask her to join my team next break.' She puts the ball on the ground and wipes her flushed face.

They reach the white door of the laboratory, where a group of pupils are already waiting for Mr Howard-Erskin, the English teacher.

'The torture lab,' someone says.

'It's not that bad, is it? Welcome again to the language lab, girls,' says Mr Howard-Erskin, pushing past them through the door.

The pupils giggle and follow him.

Zeynep whispers into Esin's ear, 'Can you imagine what Meral Hanım would have said if she'd heard us joking about her maths classroom?'

'I can. "Be respectful."'

'Erskin is the only one who can joke with us.'

Esin pulls out a chair and sits in a cubicle like the rest of the class. All of its three sides, once covered by white polystyrene, now show the wood on their edges. She places the ball under her foot then puts on her headphones. Her hair is still wet.

'We're going to switch your systems on now,' Erskin announces. 'Take out your Gatenby text books, and turn to lesson...'

The tip of Esin's pencil is broken. She looks at Zeynep, who is sitting in the next cubicle and whispers, 'Do you have a spare pencil?'

Zeynep stretches over with a sharpener in her hand.

'What are you girls doing there?'

'Just looking for a pencil sharpener, Mr Howard-Erskin.'

Esin walks to the rubbish bin in the corner and stands next to Rana, who is already sharpening her pencil with a razorblade. There's not much space. A minute later, Rana's hand slips and a few drops of blood appear on Esin's upper arm.

Rana covers her mouth with her hand. 'Oh, I'm really sorry. Does it hurt?'

Esin clutches her arm. 'It looks worse than it is.' With her hand firmly on the cut, she walks back to her desk. It stings, but was an accident.

She opens the cover of her English book. The lessons have pictures of Mr and Mrs Brown by the fire; their older children share a bedroom with a washbasin, and the maid wears a white frilly apron. Esin has never seen a fireplace in Adana nor a bedroom with a basin.

Esin isn't looking forward to the next forty-five minutes. She'd rather be in the grease-smelling food hall. She holds the ball with one foot and taps it with the other.

She twirls her pencil. A whole period of repeating words and phrases, parrot-like, and staring into the nothingness of the white cubicle feels unbearable.

Through the headphones, she hears: 'Answer the questions please. Who is serving the tea?'

All of the pupils speak at once. 'The maid is serving.'

'What has she got on the tray?'

'He has cakes.'

'Are you sure?'

'Yes.'

'*She* has cakes.'

Oh, it's so confusing. Why can't it be like Turkish? One word for both boys and girls.

'Now repeat after me. Though.'

'Dough.' Esin can't hear anybody else but Erskin.

'These.'

'Dees.'

'Those.'

'Dose.'

And it goes on. Esin looks at the white bubbles on the cubicle's walls and wonders how her brother is getting on. She bites the end of her pencil. Then her thoughts move on to the next break: who should be on her dodgeball team? They need to be equal. In that case she can't have İnci.

When sunlight floods into the lab, Esin knows the door has opened, but she can't see who has come in or gone out. Then, on her headphones, she hears Erskin's voice change. He doesn't sound like a robot anymore.

'Esin, please come out of your cubicle.'

Could he tell that she wasn't joining in with the lesson? If so, why didn't he ask her to do so?

Esin gets up, pushes in her chair and walks towards the raised platform on which his desk sits. Then she sees Mrs Bishop, the headmistress, standing by the door.

'Esin, please will you come with me?'

Mrs Bishop, in her usual green-chequered jacket, walks slowly in front. Esin checks her tie. Yes, its knot is tight in front of her collar button. Does the headmistress know that she's one of the girls who scribbled on the toilet walls?

'Your father is waiting for you.'

Esin lowers her gaze and follows Mrs Bishop until she stops at the end of the landing. Her father only comes to school for parent-teacher meetings.

She runs down the steps in twos. When she approaches the admin corridor, she stops running. Her father is standing outside the office. His hands are in the pockets of his winter coat; he doesn't smile.

'You'd better come and see your brother,' he says, and walks without removing his hands.

Esin looks down. She chews on her lower lip as they descend the main spiral staircase. His checked coat is solid like a wall. In places, paint has worn off the banister, revealing the dark metal underneath. The smell of machine oil wafts from the car repairers outside the school gates.

Yusuf Efendi's green taxi is parked at the edge of the school grounds. He is the only driver her parents use. Esin opens the door, and finds her sister already in the back seat. She is so small that Esin hadn't seen her through the window.

The drive isn't long. Esin sees cars, vans, horse carriages, carts and street vendors. A few people are already seated at Onbaşılar Kebab, their favourite Sunday lunch destination. After the loud streets they reach the calm of the hospital. Her father doesn't say anything at all.

Last night, Esin tried to make her brother laugh as she normally does by blowing air bubbles on his tummy. He smiled from his bed, but didn't make a sound. She wished to lift him, place him on her lap and play the piano. But her mother said that he was too weak to be lifted.

Yusuf Efendi parks the taxi. As Esin climbs out, she sees the white and red rose bushes in front of the hospital columns. Their fragrance invites her to remain there. As they slowly walk towards the steps leading to the main doors, Orhan Amca emerges in his white coat. Esin knows that he is the most senior doctor at the hospital. Why is he at the door?

He shakes his head.

Her father covers his face with his hands; his shoulders are hunched and shake with sobs. Esin bites the inside of her cheek until it hurts.

The drive home is so quiet. Soon after their arrival, she sees her mother come up the stairs. Next to her is Esin's uncle, holding a large wooden box.

Her mother sits by the little coffin that now lies on the dining table. Her eyes are red. Their home has many visitors. Esin wants to look inside the box but doesn't ask if she can, and no one opens its lid.

'People will come for forty days,' Meryem says; the maid knows a lot more than Esin does.

Following the funeral, friends, family and distant relatives flood their home. Esin doesn't recognise the ones with headscarves. Why do they bring food? Auntie Adile from Ankara arrives; she's the only one who smiles. Women cluster in one room, men in another. Esin wonders why.

Her mother moves her brother's shoes onto the roof.

'It's a superstition,' says Meryem.

Her brother's squidgy toy remains by her mother's bedside.

The phone rings non-stop. Esin wants to move it closer to her father but plugs it into the wrong socket and immediately pain shoots up her hand and arm. Does she jump, or does it push her away? It happens so quickly that she is not sure. She doesn't mention it to anyone – not even her little sister.

Meryem spills tea on a visitor, who yelps, 'Oh! It's burned me.'

A few days after the funeral, her mother – who hasn't spoken much – says, 'Mrs Bishop phoned. She thinks it's better if you return to school.'

'This is unusual. It must be the English tradition,' says her grandmother. The lines between her eyebrows are furrowed.

Esin isn't sure that she should really go back to school. Her mother sits by the gas heater, her hand next to a box of tissues, her gaze on the floor.

The next morning, Esin puts on her uniform: the burgundy blazer and grey pinafore dress. During the break she buys a chocolate wafer from the tuck shop. It is wrapped in gold and red cellophane. The cocoa, sugar and milk between layers of crunchy wafer tastes so good that she buys another.

Forty days later, when visitors stop coming, their house is very quiet. Esin doesn't hear her mother play music any more. The dinner arrives on the table as usual but her parents don't smile.

When they visit the grave, the pebbles under Esin's feet are uncomfortable. The brown mound of earth is smaller than the one next to it; her mother arranges red and white carnations on top.

Her father sobs. 'Bury me here when I'm gone.'

Because her mother tells Esin and her sister not to cry, Esin doesn't, but she misses her brother's giggles and the chime of the mobile above his cot.

Will her parents talk and laugh again, with music playing softly in the background?

On the forty-first day, her mother eats dinner with them. Her father peels oranges and offers them, as he used to. Do they look a little less sad?

After dinner, from the corridor, she hears her father say to her mother: 'Why did he die? We loved him more than the others.'

When her mother spots Esin standing by the door, she gasps quietly and puts her hand over her mouth.

The following day, the schoolyard is full of shouts and laughter but Esin sits by herself on a bench.

Zeynep calls to her: 'C'mon, are you not going to join in?'

Esin shakes her head. She hasn't told Zeynep that she won't play dodgeball anymore. She bites her chocolate wafer and looks at the other one resting on her lap.

James Smart is a writer from the North of England. His work has appeared in *Glimmertrain*, *Penn Review*, *Adda Stories* and elsewhere. He is a Pushcart Prize nominee and was shortlisted for the 2018 Commonwealth Writers Short Story Prize. He reads for *PANK Magazine* and tweets @notjamessmart.

notjamessmart@gmail.com

Black Sea
An extract from a novella

In Igboland, Nigeria, there is the story of the *Ogbanje*: the children who die young only to be born again in a continuing cycle, visiting renewed grief and pain upon their families.

The way to prevent the rebirth of an *Ogbanje* is to find the charm or totem they had left with their family, the object that let them return from the spirit world, their *iyi-uwa*, and set it aflame. The *iyi-uwa* is most often buried or hidden close to the family home: a charm of dove feathers; a tortoiseshell necklace; a bundle of small rabbit bones.

If the *iyi-uwa* could not be found, it is believed that female circumcision would rid the family of the curse. A wise woman would take a curved metal blade and remove the mother's clitoris; the cause, they believed, not only of *Ogbanje* but of unchecked sexual appetites, of the interest of the spirits and demons said to come to these women in their sleep.

Even then, after the burning of heirlooms and charms, and the ritual mutilation of the mother, you would not know if the cycle of *Ogbanje* was broken until the next son or daughter outlived those that had come before them, until they grew taller than their predecessors and the rest of their lives finally began.

For the fathers and children, *Ogbanje* would be over. For the mother, she would be reminded of the children she had lost every day, every time she had sex and could feel no pleasure, every time she touched herself and felt only pain.

In the West Midlands of England there are the sin-eaters: those people who come to a place of mourning to consume the sins of the dying or recently deceased. The sin-eaters arrive and eat all the guilt, shame and the filth of the dead, so the soul can be absolved of wrongdoing and pass on. When there are no bodies in need of absolution, they are avoided, shunned. When they are needed, the sin-eaters are given shelter, food and board, sleeping in the homes of those people they have absolved. They are nomads, belonging nowhere, following pestilence, battle, cataclysm.

In time, a true sin-eater comes to carry the collected sins of those they have consumed, growing heavy, slow. They harden, crystallise and fall into a spread of glassy stones. Each of them with holes bored through their centres where blood had once pumped through live veins. The pieces of the sin-eater sit in the landscape to be picked up by children, and used as witch stones to ward off nightmares or whooping cough. Hagrock, so named as all true sin-eaters were women.

In time, men have come to pose as sin-eaters, hungry for the promise of the bread, ale and sixpence they would be given for helping a soul depart. They purport to grant peace by pawning part of their own soul, and do the bare minimum before taking what they believe to be owed and leaving for the next home, never turning to stone, unable to grant absolution, instead bringing a fresh generation of devils into the world.

These stories and others like them, Eva carries with her, a record of things given, things taken away.

At Constantium Ltd, financial investment company, Eva works with men who think themselves beasts.

The executive team: an upstairs shark tank, rarely descending to the level of lesser animals. Eva thinks of them as limbs on one colossal squid, incisors and molars in one violent mouth.

Atkins: middle management, king in miniature; quaffs burnt bacon and cigarettes for breakfast while thinking himself an apex predator. When he arrives late and paces his private office, sweating, cursing and staring out through the blinds, Eva thinks, *circus lion*.

Donald: holds himself like a great ape, relaxed muscle; calm, capable occupier of space. Donald self-tans, takes all of his calls standing, is deeply afraid of human contact.

And Francis: Francis calls himself a wolf.

It's Friday night, Eva and Francis are working late, assembling a pitch for Byzantine Holdings, working on paper and whiteboards. They are the only people left in the office. They share a bottle of red wine Francis has secreted under his desk, and an eighteen-year-old scotch Eva keeps in the medicine cabinet. Music pulses through a surround sound reserved for all hand meetings, conversations with colleagues on the other side of the world.

Checking his phone and finding new messages he ignores, Francis finishes the scotch.

'You will pay for that in the morning,' Eva says, cranking the volume.

Dusty Springfield tells her lover that they don't have to say that they love her. They don't have to stay forever. She understands.

'I am paying for it right now,' Francis replies.

He drops his phone into the recycling bin and raises his voice to compete with Dusty.

Eva drinks her wine and mimes not being able to hear him.

'Half a billion dollars,' Francis says, fanning out the papers on the floor to get a bird's eye view.

'Five-hundred *million*. Over five years,' she corrects, dancing barefoot, her heels placed down on the desk like daggers.

She has selected most of the investment opportunities, scouting and vetting. She has drilled him on the pitch, written a script.

'It's your baby,' Francis says.

'I hate children.'

He pours the last of the wine and dances over to her clumsily.

'I don't believe you.'

He tries to match her movements, the gentle sway of her hips, the simple, assured angles of her arms. He fails. Francis is not a dancer.

Fleetwood Mac replaces Dusty. Stevie Nicks sings about Rhiannon, a woman taken by the wind, who rings like a bell through the night.

Francis takes Eva's hand and puts her into clumsy spin.

'We're great together,' he says, pulling closer to her.

She smells him, thinks of wet leather, the Yttrium compounds known to cause lung disease, and the investment in a rare earth material mine in Bayan Obo she signed off.

Eva completes the spin, smiles, then takes a step back.

'You'll always be my work wife, Francis,' she says, then walks over to her phone to turn down the music.

Francis falls backwards into his seat.

'We should probably stop,' he says. 'It's late. The work has been done.'

He picks up her abandoned glass and downs her drink. She begins to collect the papers, all the things they've spent the evening putting together.

'Don't worry,' Francis says, slipping off his shoes and rubbing his feet. 'I'm staying the night.'

'Abigail?'

'She wants me to be more present, then tells me she doesn't want me to come home. Mixed messages,' he says. 'All good relationships are built on communication.'

Francis takes off his suit jacket and lays his head down next to his keyboard.

'In the old days we'd sleep under our desks.'

'It's not the good old days, Francis,' Eva says. 'It never was.'

Francis drinks the last of the wine from the bottle with his eyes closed.

'Stay in a hotel.'

'I could stay with you?'

She collects her bag and coat and checks her reflection in the window overlooking London.

'Get up. One in the pub before bed.'

Blearily, Francis agrees.

She helps him put on his shoes and get into his coat. His body flops against hers.

'You smell like persimmon,' he laughs into her neck.

With him leaning against her, she struggles into her red coat.

She guides him out of the building, letting him hold onto her to keep steady.

'People will think we're lovers,' he laughs.

They pass three pubs, and a chicken shop teeming with custom.

'I don't know any of these places,' Francis says, staggering, looking in steamed windows and shaking his head.

'We don't live in the same London, Francis,' Eva says, coming to a stop and guiding him into a building.

'Your hotel,' she says, handing over her credit card to the man at reception, who is tall and thin with a gambler's stare.

The man nods and slides a pair of electronic keys across the desk.

'One is fine.'

'I won't make it up the stairs,' Francis says, reeling. 'You need to help me.'

'There is a cleaning charge for vomit.'

'He's fine.'

In the lift, Francis goes heavy, slumping his hot head into Eva's chest. She watches them in the glass ceiling.

She gets him to his room and helps him to bed.

'Stay with me awhile.'

'Goodnight, Francis.'

'A glass of water at least?'

She goes into the bathroom and pours him a glass. She looks into her eyes and pulls down the skin to expose more of the sclera, its whiteness riddled with red veins pushing the surface. She blinks and they are gone, like eels retreating to deeper waters.

In the harsh light of the hotel bathroom, her irises change shade each time she turns her head.

Returning with water, she finds Francis standing naked, soft cock emerging beneath timid brown hair, a stomach flecked with spots, doughy thighs and bird's knees.

'This is what you wanted,' he says, stepping over balled underwear and a shirt thrown off without undoing the buttons.

'Think about Abigail.'

'How can I, you looking like that?'

'I'm your friend, Francis.'

'You came back to my hotel room because you want me to fuck you,' he says, brushing his dick with the back of his hand then squeezing behind the head with his thumb, stretching himself out. 'You got drunk with me because you want me to fuck you.'

'Francis, you're in no state to fuck anyone.' She smiles, and turns the handle on the door. 'Goodnight.'

'Don't laugh at me,' he says, stumbling and falling to the floor, hitting his head on the sideboard. 'I can't bear it.'

Francis holds his head and cries into his pale chest.

At the open door, she looks out at the tan carpet of the corridor and listens to the click of lights and the urgent buzz of air conditioning, someone taking a shower in another room, canned laughter from late night TV. She looks back at Francis, the wolf, naked on the hotel room floor, holding himself, crying.

Eva closes the door.

She puts her coat and bag down and moves over to him. She puts an arm under his and lifts him onto the bed. She takes his hand away from his head and examines the wound.

'You're not bleeding.'

Francis grabs at her arm and drags it to his flaccid dick, reaching up with his mouth to find hers.

'I'm so lonely, Eva,' he says.

'Stop.'

Francis rolls backwards onto the bed, wrestling her, pushing with his mouth and hips, pulling her closer, tearing at her shirt, her tights.

'Francis, stop.'

They roll off the bed and onto the floor, he grinds down onto her, pushing his skull onto hers, his stubble chafing, breath hot.

She pushes him back, now using her strength, and clambers on top, pins his hands.

'That's the spirit,' Francis says, cock stirring.

He breaks her grip and puts a hand around her throat.

Eva's eyes go black. Her back arches and fur pushes to the surface. Her legs snap back and split her skirt, strong legs covered in matted black hair, tearing through. Her fingers jerk in their sockets, thumbs crack and twist into sharp claws. Her ribs curl, breasts spread, cunt folds, a tail splinters from the base of her spine, unfurls free, spearing her underwear. Eva grows larger, shoulders moving, shredding her shirt. Her nose breaks, remoulding into a long snout. Her mouth opens wide with pain, long sharp canines pushing from her gums. She breathes heavy through the change, the soft skin of her face reconfiguring, becoming, throwing heat, new muscle, everything alive with fur.

Francis shrieks, pulling away, pissing scared onto his stomach and the carpet. And then, as a wolf, Eva tears off the fingers of his left hand.

Amelia Vale grew up in Cambridge, England, the proud owner of an extensive flannel wardrobe.

She is currently working on a collection of international, love-themed short stories titled *Roast Novel*, from which her work 'Commas' comes. Her writing centres on the lonely, the fantastic and the queer.

amelia.gvale@gmail.com

Commas
A short story

One day when I was young, but not so young, my mother and I were parked up at a red light. We had been at that red light for so long she had turned the car engine off.

I looked at her from my spot in the passenger seat, suddenly, and I said, 'Have you ever had an abortion?'

'Sorry?' she said to me.

I asked her again.

This was a hot summer. We had all the windows rolled down, front and back. We had the sunroof open. My mother always liked to keep a bag of toffees in the glove compartment of her black Peugeot; unwrapped and ready to chew. These toffees had melted and reformed so many times in the heat that they were little more than a sugar lump, and this lump gave the car a sickly sweet smell.

'Yes,' my mother answered me. 'I had one once. It was a little boy. At least I think it was, I felt it was a boy.'

'What does a boy feel like?' I said.

'Heavier,' said my mother. She licked her lips. She had a film of sweat balanced on her blonde moustache, and patches under her arms. 'It's hard to explain. What happened was, I went to the doctor and they gave me a pill to take. The next day, I had another pill to put inside of myself.'

'How long ago was this?' I said.

'A few years. They kept asking me if I was sure. I said I was very sure.'

'Did you not want him?'

'It's not that simple.'

'Isn't it?'

My mother shook her head. The cars ahead of us crept forwards by the inch, but we stayed still behind the traffic lights. There were surface pools of melted tarmac on the ground, bright like oil slicks. The grass on the approaching verge was hard and dead. The truck in front had a bumper sticker that went: *Two Beers and I'm Gay*. 'I wanted him,' said my mother. 'I still want him now. Sometimes I lie awake and think about how different things could have been, but I don't regret it.'

'You never met the father,' she said. 'It was a short-term thing.' It was her turn to look at me. 'Why do you ask?'

'Because Katy B had one,' I said. 'She told me at that party you took me to last week that she had one in secret and never told her parents. She said she had to get the bus back home afterwards and felt sick to her stomach, like she'd eaten bad Chinese or something, and she had to get a special doctor's note for school. She had to get one alone. She almost threw up on the bus.'

'She's very brave,' said my mother.

'And because we watched a video at school of a woman getting it sucked out of her, like with a hoover.'

'Sometimes it happens like that,' said my mother.

I leant back in my seat and rested a hand on my crotch. 'Every time I hoover from now on, I'm going to think about that video.'

My mother laughed. Then she told me how, after the second pill of her abortion, the one she put inside of herself, she passed my almost-brother right away. The lining of her womb slipped out like jelly. 'He was like a little pea,' she said. 'A clot. A full stop without a sentence to go along, if you can imagine it, only that's wrong, because he's been more of a comma ever since. Sometimes I look at a comma on a piece of paper, and randomly I find myself thinking of him.'

My mother reached over into the glove compartment and broke a piece of toffee off for each of us, slimy and dark.

'How about you then?' she said. 'Have you had one?'

'No,' I told her truthfully, speaking with my mouth full. Back then when I was young, but not so young, it was the truth. 'I have a plan,' I said. 'My plan is that if I ever get pregnant I'm going to keep it no matter what, whether it's a boy, or a girl, or anything.'

The traffic light above us finally changed from red to green. My mother turned on the engine and we passed the crossing at a crawl, driving forwards to meet the road ahead.

'It's not that simple,' she said.

'Isn't it?'

Melissa Wan writes short fiction. Her story *The Husband and the Wife Go to the Seaside* (Bluemoose Books, 2018) will be reprinted in Salt's *Best British Short Stories 2019*. She was awarded the Crowdfunded BAME Writers' Scholarship to study at UEA, and is currently working on her first collection of stories.

melissa.brakel@gmail.com

Rest in Peace, Madame Wong

A short story

I was alone, but at least I'd brought the plant pot. Everyone in the hide had something with them: either another person or a pair of binoculars with which to look at the birds. Some had both. The man beside me on the bench was alone but to compensate he had an enormous camera on a tripod. Again and again he bowed his head to the rim of the viewfinder as though in an act of contrition.

I whispered to the plant on my lap, which was supposedly a cherry blossom bonsai, but which was really just a crooked stem in a pot far too big for it. It felt natural to treat it like a baby. I said things like, *Today is a beautiful day, won't you come out to see it? The sun is shining just for you.* Its trunk stood an inch above the soil before diverging into three branches. These were covered in smaller shoots that reached towards the sky. I hoped it would eventually flower, imagined the surprise of frothy white petals. I'd heard that plants respond to attention and intention as much as they do water and sunlight. We do them a disservice thinking they merely need the basics. As if humans could survive only on food and water! I'd read online about a woman who nursed a sick fern back to life by cradling its pot and thinking the word 'love' over and over. *Love love love.* Soon the rusty fronds were luscious and green. The power of the mind.

The plant was not actually mine, but Madame Wong's. 'Madame Wong's' might sound like a massage parlour but the name belonged to a real woman. It was written on her letterbox. She lived across the hall, a few doors down. I first met her one afternoon when coming back from a walk around St John's Gardens. She was struggling down the stairs, wearing yellow rubber gloves and carrying a stack of three potted plants. I asked if she needed a hand.

'I refuse to throw them out,' she wheezed. Her perfect English took me by surprise.

'Where are you taking them?' I said.

'I want to put them outside because I don't get much light in my place.'

'You know they'll probably get stolen.'

She laughed, revealing a mouth studded with gold teeth. When I took the top two pots, she put the bottom one down and sank into an impressive squat to catch her breath. The oily black hair which had made her appear younger from a distance was up close interspersed with white, and her face was abundant with lines. Eyeliner spilled into the creases around her eyes.

'I'm on the side that gets sun during the day,' I said. 'If you wanted to leave one with me for a while.' I didn't offer to take them all as I had little confidence I could look after multiple living things at the same time. In my fridge there was always something hardened or collapsed under a coat of green and white fur.

'You would take one?' she asked.

I looked into the pots in my hands. Both were sad, but something inside me responded to the one on the left. It had potential. I imagined speaking to it, thought of the secrets I might divulge.

'They are both blossom,' she said. 'Quiet and nice-smelling.'

'I can't promise anything, but I could try with this one.'

Together we walked back up the stairs, carrying the pots easily between the two of us. Luckily, I always kept my apartment primed in case of visitors. The last time anyone had set foot inside was three years ago, when the plumber came to fix a leak in the base of the toilet. This solitude wasn't intentional. It was just the way things had turned out. But high on my list of fears was not being prepared. The idea of someone knocking on my door and finding my expulsions – dead hairs, toenail clippings, bits of food; all those things that collect in corners over time – motivated me to keep the flat impeccable. I'd long thrown out all knickers I wouldn't want to be caught dead in, and I didn't own pyjamas. Instead I wore a flattering outfit which was also suitable for sleeping. This way I was always prepared for an intruder: most likely a thief or a rapist, if not both.

I knew which was Madame Wong's flat because a year or so ago someone had written *No More Japs* in black pen across her door. At the time I'd hoped she didn't speak English well enough to know what it meant, but as we walked by I asked if she couldn't get her husband to remove it.

'I don't have a husband.'

'Oh.' I knew a Tony Wong and presumed they were married. 'So you don't know Tony Wong from the Residents' Association?'

'There are a lot of Wongs in the world,' she said, 'but also a lot of whites.'

The joke was well-practised and she watched for my laugh. I smiled, a little embarrassed, and asked if she wanted me to try and clean it.

'No, I'm not Japanese so I don't bother about it.'

I opened the door to my flat and Madame Wong took off her flip-flops before stepping inside. Seeing this woman in my living room, I felt my years of hard work beginning to pay off. The surfaces shone and a stream of sunlight was at that very moment coming through the kitchen window and onto the worktop, as though recommending the best spot.

'Shall I put it here?' I asked.

Madame Wong eyed the plant and nodded.

'I can give you a tour of the flat if you'd like to know the kind of home your plant is coming into?'

We moved to the bedroom where I gestured to the window seat, its cushions plumped. 'This room gets the sun in the afternoon, so it's the perfect place to sit and meditate.' I wanted her to see me in the lotus position, palms open to the world. The window was on a slight gap so fresh air could circulate, and there was always a scarf placed just so on the edge of the bed, almost but not quite touching the carpet. Every morning I made sure to pull the duvet taut, but I always tossed my robe over the Japanese screen, casually, as though I'd been in a rush getting dressed.

'Sorry about the mess,' I said.

'I see you are also a lone bird,' she said, in a manner I felt to be approving. Then, as often happens when people have what they want from you, I felt her starting to withdraw. 'Do you want a cup of tea before you go?' I asked.

'That's OK,' she said.

'OK. Well, you can come back to visit your plant whenever you want.'

'I will come and water maybe once every six, seven days, OK.' And with that she walked to the front door, holding up her gloved hand in farewell.

In the end I brewed Madame Wong's cup of tea, then let it grow cold on the table. As it turned out, the milk was sour, so I was glad she hadn't accepted. Over the next few days I kept her plant on the sill and made sure to accommodate it. It was a living thing deserving of the same respect as any other living thing. If I had the radio on, I kept it at just the right volume so the plant could hear but without being disturbed. No doubt their ears are more sensitive than ours.

On one of these days, when I opened my front door to air the kitchen after cooking, I smelled cigarettes. I stuck my head into the corridor and found a young man smoking outside Madame Wong's flat.

'I'm sorry, but you're not allowed to smoke there,' I said. I told him it was a fire hazard, though I was mainly concerned about the smell.

He looked at me, then licked his fingers and pinched the cigarette tip until it died.

'Are you looking for Madame Wong?' I asked.

He shook his head and before I could ask any more, he said, 'She's dead.'

He disappeared inside her flat. The door closed gently behind him, then clicked shut. *No More Japs.*

The hide was silent as an empty church, but without the judgement. An aeroplane slowly marked a white trail across the empty sky and the reed beds shone gold in the late afternoon sun. I'd brought the plant here because it was grieving and I know it's impossible to grieve in a big city, where nothing stops, not even noise, although you feel everything ought to grind to a standstill.

The man to my right asked if I wanted to take a look through his camera. He smiled with childlike innocence and I said it was nice to see someone enjoying themselves so much.

'There's just so much going on,' he thrilled. When I shuffled in closer, his wax jacket had a sour smell, but I could forgive kind strangers almost anything. The view through the camera showed me the world in HD. Ducks dipped forward into the water, then bobbed up again in a movement I found hugely gratifying to watch.

'It's wonderful,' I said.

'Now look at this.' He turned the camera a little to the right and encouraged me to lean down again. As soon as I did, I saw the bird: its long neck and snow-white feathers. Two slender plumes grew from the back of its crown and its eye was looking straight at me.

'What is it?' I asked.

'That's a little egret,' he said. 'Cousin of the heron.'

'She's got very cheeky eyes.'

'You've done well to recognise that's a female.'

I didn't tell him I had the sense the bird was Madame Wong. Down to the bright yellow feet, like she was still wearing her washing-up gloves. Something in her gaze felt accusatory, and I held a little tighter to the pot. Though I read sadness too, in the hunch of her shoulders, and I wondered if she'd come back to see her plant: the thing she hadn't had the chance to say goodbye to. As though in response to my thought, Madame Wong started to flap her wings.

'What's she doing?' I asked, leaning away from the camera. Sweat prickled on the back of my neck.

'Oh, just birds being birds,' he said. 'Here, she's getting ready to fly.'

I felt relief as she lifted into the air, graceful, weightless. Her feathers caught the sun and the light winked at us as she flew away.

When the plant flowered, it was not a cherry blossom but a citrus bonsai, which repaid my patience in miniature orange fruits. I admired them, sometimes with my fingers, but I could never water without the thought of Madame Wong and her stare from the other side, which seemed to me now to have been almost pleading. I knew I would eventually need to give the plant back, for her to enjoy in the afterlife. I wasn't convinced there was such a thing as an afterlife, but if there was, I wouldn't want her to be alone.

I found out the name of the cemetery in which she was buried. She was easy to find as her headstone was clean, as yet unmarked by time. I couldn't read the Chinese characters but recognised her in the memorial photo on the granite. She was much younger in the picture – plump-lipped and dewy – but her eyes had the same vibrancy as they'd had in life.

I put the flowers in front of the headstone and said, 'I'll come and water maybe once every six, seven days, OK.'

Bethany Wright is from Buckinghamshire. She studied French and German at New College, Oxford, and has lived in Paris, Frankfurt and Madrid. Before coming to UEA, she worked in publishing for five years, editing books on art, cookery and natural history. She is working on her first novel.

bethany.wright05@gmail.com

Dusk
An extract from a novel

He sees her before she sees him. That means he has a few moments to prepare himself, to rehearse his words, to place his body. Luke's never considered the possibility of meeting her like this. He's imagined passing her on the street, stopping dead so the people walking behind have to check their step and flow around him. He's thought about how he'll keep his gaze on her as she draws near, how she'll glance up and in that moment something will flicker in her eyes, too briefly for him to tell if it's happiness or disgust.

But he's never imagined meeting Helen in a crowded student living room, with damp walls shedding their skin in magnolia scales. He hasn't pictured himself sitting against a thick-barred radiator as she slides into view in the doorway. Her hair is shorter, its tips just brushing her collarbones. Her cheeks are flushed from the cold. She shrugs her bag off her shoulder, one long careless movement that sends recognition flooding through him.

A few of the others break off their conversations to lob a casual greeting across the room. They don't suck uncomfortable breaths past their teeth, don't slide glances in his direction to catch the colour rising in his face. They don't know there's anything for them to react to.

Sam jumps up to pour her a glass of wine. He obscures Luke's view for a second but when he sits down again she's still there, perched on the edge of the sofa.

Then she sees him. She pauses, the glass raised halfway to her lips. Her face tightens. Her eyes are trained on him. There's no message in them; she's watching him rather than meeting his gaze, as if he's an animal and she's waiting to see if he'll attack.

Sam looks from Helen to Luke.

'Of course, you guys haven't met,' he says. 'Luke's on the master's with me. Luke, this is my housemate, Helen.'

Luke shifts, feeling faintly ridiculous on the floor with his knees poking up. He's never seen Helen from this angle before, him bundled on the worn carpet and her raised above him on the sofa's fraying arm. It was always the other way round.

He's about to speak, although he's not sure what he'll say, when Helen gives him a smile.

'Nice to meet you,' she says.

Her eyes glide away. Surely it's not possible she didn't recognise him. He hasn't changed that much in the past four years, although he must look a bit different in his jeans and jumper. Younger, perhaps. He must look younger to her now that she's older, now that people would think of them as roughly the same age. Strange how a few years have shrunk the gap between them.

He should be glad Helen's keeping her head resolutely turned away. It gives him a chance to stare, to grow accustomed to the sight of her after so long. He's pictured her face so many times that he's made it vaguer, rubbed the edges off. He's forgotten what she looks like in motion, her lips forming words, her eyes flicking from one person to the next. The way her chewed fingers scoop her hair behind one ear, the creases that draw in around her lips when she sips her wine.

It takes Luke a few seconds to realise the girl next to him has asked a question. He searches his memory for her name, the one she told him only a few minutes before. Tess. She nudges him and holds out a beer, asking again if he wants another. He nods and she passes it. Taking a long pull from the bottle, Luke tries to focus on what Tess is saying, but his mind is buzzing with the knowledge that Helen is there. Just a few feet away from him. Almost close enough to touch.

Helen feels a wash of relief as Luke's gaze breaks away. Her whole body was heavy with him, her jaw locked in the grip of his eyes. She wanted to dip her chin and veil herself with her hair, but she can't do that any more. It's been years since her hair was that long.

At least he's looked away now. She can let herself breathe again, but not too deeply. He's still there, sitting against the far wall. Those hands with their lace of scars gripping his beer bottle, those long legs creeping across the floor. He takes up so much space in the room.

He leans forward to listen to Tess and Helen feels her body respond. Just the slightest shift, as if she needs to keep the distance between them constant. He rests the beer on his knee, then cups it in both hands. Then he places it on the floor and twists his fingers together. He never could learn to keep still.

Sam launches into a complicated story about one of his lecturers. She tries to listen but there is too much noise. Everyone is laughing and drinking and talking over each other. The heat from their bodies presses down on her skin. She risks another glance at Luke.

His face looks wrong against the backdrop of the chipped radiator. So familiar and so startling. His hair is longer than it used to be, long enough that it's just started to curl. There's a blur of stubble on his jaw. The light flashes off his glasses so she can't see his eyes.

He shouldn't be here. He doesn't belong in her living room, with her friends, in her city. He couldn't let her have this one place to herself.

Helen sips her wine and focuses on Sam. But every time she blinks, she sees the look that flitted across Luke's face when she pretended not to know him. Not surprise or disbelief, but hurt. Injury. He has no right to look so wounded.

Luke takes a gulp of beer and it lingers in his mouth, prickling at the broken gum where a wisdom tooth is coming in. He's drinking too fast but it gives his hands something to do. The tide of alcohol tugs at him, dragging him further out. The voices around him seem blurry.

Tess has turned to the guy on her other side and started an impassioned debate about veganism. Luke could try to hang on to the fringes of their conversation but he can't summon the energy. Instead he looks at Helen.

The wine has left a ruby shade on her lips. She presses them into a quick smile. Tighter than the smile he remembers, but still it teases out the dimple in her cheek. The one that always gave her away when she was about to laugh at him.

She and Sam are sitting close, their shoulders brushing. Snatches of their conversation drift through the chatter.

'He sounds like a right little shit,' Sam says.

He places a hand on Helen's arm, a touch so casual neither of them seems to notice it. Luke draws his fingers into his palm.

'I think he's just testing me,' Helen says. 'They said to go in strict and relax once you've earned their respect, but it's hard to be stern when they're only a few years younger than you.'

'You'll get there. No one's expecting you to have classroom control down straight away.'

Helen shrugs, the movement coaxing out hollows above her collarbones. Deep in Luke's stomach his beer is swilling round, uneasy, like a sink that can't quite drain.

He's looking at her again. Helen can feel the familiar weight of his gaze settling around her shoulders. Maybe she should just talk to him. Stand up, take those few steps across the room to where he's sitting. Except then she'll have to speak first, and she hasn't yet worked out what she wants to say. If only Luke would approach her, start trying to explain, his words would give her a foothold to push off from. But he doesn't move.

The room is too loud. It bristles with bodies. She can't pin down her thoughts with all this noise. Maybe if she goes somewhere quiet. It was always easy to talk when it was just the two of them. There was a rhythm to their conversations, an instinct for when to speak and when to be silent. All those evenings together, cocooned in the fading light. Maybe if she can get him alone, she'll know what to say.

Sam heads to the kitchen to fetch another bottle and Helen slips out. She meets Luke's eye as she goes. It's an invitation. He must know it. Surely, even after all these years, he knows how to read her face.

She steps into the scrubby garden, with its weeds thrusting between paving slabs. The sagging fence drops splinters onto the grass and a pile of leaves moulders quietly in the corner. She shivers. She should have grabbed her coat but that would have drawn attention to her departure. Instead she pulls her lighter from the pocket of her jeans and lets the snap of its flame warm her fingers. She lights a cigarette and inhales.

She's only smoked socially since coming to university, only when the huddle outside the party is more interesting than the one indoors. It seems futile to stick up two nicotine-stained fingers if her mum isn't there to see them. But here in the cold garden, she savours the rasp in her lungs.

The door opens and closes behind her. Three footsteps draw him level and he stops, hands in his pockets.

'I didn't know you smoked.'

She catches the laugh that surges in her throat. It stays there, smoke swirling around it.

'You're not going to tell me it's bad for me, are you?'

Somehow she can't find the right way to drive a distance between them. Luke hasn't moved but it feels like he's stepped closer.

'You're training to be a teacher,' he says.

The words sound like an accusation.

'I thought you wanted to work in theatre. You wanted to start your own production company.'

Helen tries to make her laugh soft, as if she's only just remembering a dream that faded a long time ago.

'That's right, I did say I wanted to work in theatre.' She shrugs. 'Who has any idea what they want when they're eighteen?'

She means it as a dismissal of herself but he flinches. An image sparks in her mind: Luke standing at the front of the classroom, one hand stretched out to point at the board. He's not looking at her. The girl in the row behind is asking a question and his eyebrows are slightly raised as he listens. His tie is snug at his collar but later he'll loosen it, one finger hooked into the knot as he eases it away from his throat.

Rebecca Yolland is a teacher and currently runs workshops on creative thinking for science students. She has worked as a film editor for the BBC and ITV and in various roles around the world for the International Red Cross and Red Crescent Societies and the United Nations.

beccayolland@hotmail.com

Herding
Extract from the opening of a novel

Agnes woke to church bells ringing in the distance and wondered if the drought would ever end. Her head hurt, her legs ached, her stomach carried its own pain.

She had been walking for days now. Six days if she counted back through the nights. Six days walking forward with her mind, thinking what to say when she arrived, wondering about the look on Margaret's face as they met.

Two days it was since food had passed her lips. She had fasted before but never like this. Her body was shutting down and her mind beginning to open on a world where colours fed her and the walking carried her.

The hills built. She fell easily, often, and the angel of time passed over before she got up again. Paths took her as they chose and she trusted in them as she moved deeper and deeper into the forest. Insects rattled like a cloud of seeds flung into the canopy. Birds grew new feathers in secret and no longer sang. She remembered the same wary silence from childhood after the tiller's clacker had startled crows into the air.

Then, the dog came: a dark shadow in the rustle of last year's leaves. It was fast and lithe and carried its hips high as it hurtled down the bank, pulling the dry earth away from the roots of the trees.

Agnes firmed her stance and braced her feet wide against the soil. With one foot a little in front of the other, her chin lowered and her arms limp, she willed herself not to move.

Close now. Closer. Almost on her. There was a smell of fur and animal force. She could see the spittle on the dog's gums and the white of its teeth. The flap of tongue shocked her like a naked man.

Agnes looked around for a rock.

The dog leapt high and landed at her feet, forelegs stretched out and toes splayed; growling, then barking, then panting heavily in the heat. Agnes felt sweat run down her own back.

'You sorry thing,' she said, holding her hand out for sniffing. 'Too hot for a coat of fur.'

Folding further into herself, she listened to the dog nosing against her, butting into her with wet life. She lifted up her rosary beads so they knocked against themselves.

'You wanting to play?'

The dog barked softly. Agnes spun in a circle and it raced round her. She wanted to laugh but she caught herself before she did, and instead peered towards the shadows. A dog meant men on the move or a cottage nearby: the trees were uprights behind which anyone might hide.

She bent down. The dog barked again and began to beg.

'I've nothing for you.'

He ran to and fro. He ran away from the path and down the bank to the stream where he licked at the stones. He ran back to her, jumping up and marking her with dirt as high as her muslin neckerchief, his nails sharp against her.

'Careful now.'

She stood up, each movement an ache and the hunger hard in her belly. She turned slowly, scanning the trees, looking forward along the path. An aisle ahead. Shadows like falling ash.

'Where's your master, then?'

She walked. The dog came with her, his nose wet in the loose cup of her hand. The path was studded with jewels: the bright blue sheen of dung beetles like the riches of church. She tried not to step on God's creatures, but her feet had separated themselves from her mind.

The sheep were lying down in the shade but some had spread themselves across the path or in the puddle of the stream and the sound of them together – chewing and grinding teeth like the very old – jolted her with loneliness.

Agnes knew she had to keep moving, following the forest path until it opened out to the fields beyond, until those fields became the town she had been travelling towards for days, until she reached Margaret.

The sheep were restless as the dog moved amongst them. Agnes continued to put one foot in front of the other and the dog helped her. She noticed the little cloth boots covering some of the sheep hoofs, like the wrappings of her own feet. It made her wince again. She pulled her coif further down her forehead, aware of the dirt, and straightened the muslin across her chest. She lowered her eyes and walked.

It was a hundred paces through the sheep that she felt the men's eyes upon her. She was aware of them, in a group in the dappled shade, banded round a cloth-wrapped pie and a jug. The men wore their clothes easy with grime and the black curls of their hair fell free. One man lay casually propped on an elbow with a knee up and jigging as he drank. Another was a boy but already his eyes had that faraway stare of a drover – the lowering of eyebrows – as he appraised her. The third had a red beard, strange against his black hair. This one held a knife and a sheep's foot in his hands: he clamped the sheep down with the weight of his thigh as he dug into the frog of the hoof. There was another dog with them, sleeping at their feet.

'God be with you,' she said, as she kept her eyes on the path and picked her pace faster. She thought of the pie.

The first dog nipped at her heels. The drinking man laughed. The path was taking her closer to him. She could not avoid it. She saw the tankard swing in his hand and saw him place it carefully down. He turned to the others and talked in a language she did not understand.

'Lass like you out in the wood,' he said to her, as he stood in one swift movement. 'God be good.' He hitched at the tie of his trousers and shrugged his hips comfortably. 'Out all alone, without a man?' He clicked his fingers at the boy who jumped quickly to his feet in answer.

Agnes kept her eyes on the red-bearded man as the other two began to flank her. He slapped at the side of the sheep he had been wrestling and, once it had veered off into the flock, he got up slowly. His eyes were steady as they travelled to the faces of his companions and then settled on Agnes. She heard a movement behind her and the sound of hawking spit. Her eyes flitted this way and that: a bird tracking a route through a bush.

She felt her ribs tighten. She lowered her chin and braced her body.

On his feet the red-bearded man was the largest. He still held the knife loosely in his palm.

'Hup,' said the man. 'Hup hup.'

The first dog moved away from her. The second barked and jumped to its feet. All three men were laughing, and the laughter came to her like the deep sounding of a well. The dogs began to circle. Noses down and legs splayed, they jumped at the sheep.

Agnes longed for a cup of water. She longed to drink and drink and to pour the water across her face until she felt the soothing coolness of being washed.

The sheep were getting to their feet, back legs first, rumps in the air, running unsteadily away from the dogs. The rattle of the insects stopped, the noises of the forest floor expanded. She looked at where the maggots writhed at the sheep's tails and she swallowed dry. Her hands formed into fists. The sheep were circling round and round her, coming together, bodies blocking her. A small number at first and then more as the fear took them and they skittered from the dogs, bumping into each other, into her. The men were on their feet, holding sticks wide, hupping and whistling their dogs and their herd. Driving them hard.

Her legs were weak against the strength of the sheep. The muscle in her thighs met the muscle in theirs. More and more, hundreds of them, the uprights of the trees springing from a sea of wool. She knew she must stay on her feet.

As she wobbled, the men laughed, their faces red with power and beer. She turned her back on them. If she could reach a full-grown trunk she could hold to it. She nudged her legs forward, keeping her arms up. The sheep jostled but they responded to her, backing away just enough for her to move forward. Their bleating reached a pitch. She pushed on, her stomach stabbing, her legs straining, her feet screaming when the sheep trod on them. Her skirts caught between their bodies and she was pulled this way and that. She grabbed at the cloth to get herself free. The men whistled at her through their laughter and these whistles were new notes. She drove forward and forward until she reached a tree.

She caught it, felt the rough bark and turned against it for support. The bark ran its fingers down her back. The sheep still pressed round her but the tree held her straight as the roots beneath her feet twisted her shoes and made her blisters weep.

She looked out over the writhing wool at the men re-forming their group. Two of them bent over, laughing hard. Still distant for now.

The bone at the back of her skull rested against the tree. She could feel the muscles tight in front of her ears. Her jaw was set as a man's. Her blood ran through her, hardening now, like sap.

She caught the stare of the red-bearded man and held it.

The first man laughed and laughed, hanging on to the boy and leaning on his stick. 'Just a bit a fun, girl.'

Her focus did not shift.

The bearded man put his knife away, then wiped his lips with a dirty sleeve. 'We have no need of you,' he said, 'after a night in town. God be with you on your way.'

The other two hefted their packs and walked by, settling into the fluid gait of years on the road.

The third man put his hand to his mouth and whistled loud and long. The dogs ran, and the sheep loosened their form around her. She watched them all go up the path, taking the way she had come. The friendly dog rounded back and bunted once into her skirts before sprinting off. She traced the grooves of the tree with her fingertips and listened until the sound of hoofs had faded away.

Acknowledgements

This anthology contains work written by the 2019 cohort of UEA's MA and MFA in Creative Writing: Prose Fiction. We are very grateful for the support of the UEA School of Literature, Drama and Creative Writing in partnership with Egg Box Publishing, without whom this anthology would not have been possible.

We would like to thank our course directors Philip Langeskov, Naomi Wood, and Trezza Azzopardi, alongside our other workshop tutors Andrew Cowan, Giles Foden, Jean McNeil, Amita Murray, and Julianne Pachico. We deeply appreciate all of their insights.

We are thankful to the authors who have contributed to this year's Masterclasses – Diana Evans, Sabrina Mahfouz, and Chris Power – as well as 2019's visiting UNESCO fellow, the knowledgeable and enthusiastic Preti Taneja.

Huge thanks to Nathan Hamilton at the UEA Publishing Project alongside Rachel Hore, Emily Benton and Sarah Gooderson for their help managing, designing and proofreading this anthology. Thanks also to the editorial committee: Judith Khan and Jon Platten (Biography and Creative Non-Fiction); Poppy Kleiser and Deshawn McKinney (Poetry); Amber Higgins and Jasmin Kirkbride (Prose Fiction); and Taylor Biedler (Scriptwriting). Thanks also to our hardworking Prose Fiction editors Fearghal Hall, Tess O'Hara, Ceci Mazzarella, Tasha Ong, Rebecca Sollom, Stephanie Tam and Melissa Wan.

With grateful thanks to all of the donors who contribute to the scholarships that support our writers, including: the Annabel Abbs Scholarship, the Booker Prize Foundation Scholarship, the Curtis Brown Award, the David Higham Award, the International Excellence Scholarships, the Kowitz Scholarship, the Malcolm Bradbury Memorial Scholarship, the Miles Morland Foundation African Scholarship, the Santander Scholarship, the Seth Donaldson Memorial Bursary, and the UEA Crowdfunded BAME Writers' Scholarship.

Lastly, of course, huge gratitude to all of our fellow students for your friendship, patience, kindness, and margin notes – here's to your future writing.

UEA MA Creative Writing Anthologies: Prose Fiction, 2019

First published by Egg Box Publishing, 2019
Part of UEA Publishing Project Ltd.

International © 2019 retained by individual authors

A CIP record for this book is available from the British Library
Printed and bound in the UK by Imprint Digital

Designed by Emily Benton Book Design
emilybentonbookdesigner.co.uk

Proofread by Sarah Gooderson

Distributed by NBN International
10 Thornbury Road Plymouth
PL6 7PP
+44 (0)1752 202301
e.cservs@nbninternational.com

ISBN: 978-1-911343-69-1